Velvet Rose

By Leonora Morrison

Leonora Morrison

I am a graduate of both the University of Ulster and Queens University, Belfast graduating with an MA in Eighteenth Century Studies in 2008. I have a keen interest in history, art and culture pertaining to this period. I have always been drawn to old books it is an amazing feeling to be in an old library surrounded by so much history and creativity.

I studied eighteenth century erotica as part of MA course and I feel it has evolved into something completely different in this modern age. This is in the main part due to the speed and changes created by the internet. The trend for online dating instead of literally going out and bumping into people has created opportunity and yet at the same time denies what may be called 'old fashioned courtship'. To some romance is dead. In research for my first novel *The Bed and the Bookcase* I researched a lot online. The book combined the style of online blogging with my fascination of books and erotic literary taste.

It was after almost a years planning I sat down and started to write *Red Velvet Rose*. I had researched everything I wished to include and had around twenty pages written when everything changed. I kept reading up about different events that had happened in Belfast throughout its colourful and often bloody history. When I stumbled across an article featured in the *Northern Whig*. This article regarding the finding of several severed heads and bones while digging foundations had me fascinated. Those who know me well and they are few know I am fascinated by the gothic and macabre. My imagination started to work overtime and a years worth of planning started to dissolve into nothing but daydreams. *The Cult of the Red Dragon* suddenly moved to Belfast and around it grew a tale of fear, tragedy, love, lust, murder and mayhem. Just a typical day in the history of our colourful city some may say. Forget what you know, forget what you think you know because none of us know what really has happened in the past. History is written by those in control the winners of wars, the survivors not the losers. We know what we are lead to believe and what others wish us to think. It's time to think outside the box to imagine and wonder, what really happened in Victorian Belfast and indeed at any other time. Even today societies exist here without the knowledge of the government, groups within groups and a social hierarchy with a hidden past. The book is based on true events and this is how these events have played out in my mind.

Printed in the United Kingdom

First Printing, 2018

ISBN 978-1-9995918-0-9

Contact via Instagram: LeonoraMorrison or
Leonoramorrison@hotmail.com

Often it is said that one conversation can change the way you view everything. It is not something I would have believed, that moment in a million years............. After that moment there was no one else i could dedicate *Red Velvet Rose* to... you know who you are......

'That night in the castle in the clouds surrounded by stars and a million lights, you asked me to stay...........I'm still there'.

The Sick Rose by William Blake

O Rose thou art sick

That invisible worm

That flies in the night

In the howling storm

Has found out thy bed

Of crimson Joy

And his dark secret love

Does thy life destroy

I have throughout the story made reference to places that existed and events which happened in Victorian Belfast. Many of these buildings still exist today such as *The Crown bar* and *the Poor House in Donegal Street*. Many of the theatres in Belfast such as those in Albert Street and Smithfield did not see the nineteenth century. They were replaced by what is now The Grand Opera House. I have used some of the buildings at times they did not exist for purposes of the story. The correct dates of buildings and events are as follows.

1307 – *The Baphomet* first emerges as a form of ideal or deity supposedly worshipped by *The Templars*. The use of the term became popular again the nineteenth century and can be associated with freemasonry.

15th Century – Dragons have throughout history held a variety of symbolic meanings. The dragon is and was mainly associated with Chinese mythology of which it maintained a Royal position often due to its protection of the Chinese people from inclement weather. In other sources dragons were a form of evil spirit which had to be destroyed by a saint or hero such as George or Perseus. Many painters have used the theme of dragons in their works. The dragon was also used as a symbol of protection from Vlad Drakul in the late 15th century an early 16th century, he is more commonly known today as Dracula. 'The Order of the Dragon' or *Drachenorden* was founded by the King of Hungary in 1408 and later lead by the Holy Roman Emperor to fight the enemies of Christianity. They were mostly supported by the political nobility who were fond of corruption and murder.

1531 – Act of Parliament to deal with problem of unemployed (thewildpeakwordpress.com).
In 1531 an Act of Parliament allowed licences for begging to be granted to the impotent, and ordered a whipping for all other mendicants. Five years later, in the year of the suppression of the lesser monasteries, Parliament, finding the unemployed still alive, decided to deal more radically with the problem. So on the first conviction of unemployment all vagrants, men, and women alike, were to be whipped; for the second offence they were to be mutilated; and on the third conviction they were to be hanged as felons. This Act of 1536 was rigidly enforced and thousands of unemployed men and women suffered the full penalty of the law.

And still the "unemployed problem" remained unsolved, so that it was said that only by sterner measures and greater severity could the question be settled.

Therefore, in 1547, the first year of Edward VI., an Act was passed selling the unemployed into slavery. For a first conviction branding and two years of slavery was ordered for the unemployed vagrant; the "slave" was to be beaten and chained by his master, and for running away he was to be further branded and adjudged a "slave" for ever. Death as a felon was the penalty for a third conviction.

1754– *The Brown Linen Hall* was opened in the site of what is now *St Anne's Cathedral.*

1757-1827 *William Blake* poet, artist and known occultist

1774 – *Clifton House* was officially opened as a poorhouse. It is now one of Belfast oldest surviving buildings. When it was built it was situated in open countryside at the head of Donegal Street. The surrounding area was not sold for development until the 1790s.

1793 – *The Theatre Royal* at 1-3 Arthur Street is opened. It is replaced in 1871 only to have the interiors destroyed by fire in June 1881. It is again refurbished in 1915; the building was demolished in 1961.

1828 – *Belfast Botanic Garden opens* containing many exotic plants from the southern hemisphere, including *prunes lusitanica* also known as *Portuguese laurel* which contains cyanide. The Dome was added in 1852 it was designed by Charles Lanyon who was responsible for designing a lot of the high profile buildings in Belfast at the time, including *Crumlin Road Gaol and Courthouse.* The upkeep of the gardens became too much for the shareholders and the garden was sold to the Belfast Corporation which later reopened the gardens in 1895.

1840 – Legislation is passed to prevent the use of 'Climbing boys' to clean chimneys. This could not have come soon enough as there were many reports of boys being burnt to death while cleaning fires because the residence were cold and didn't want the fire dampened. However, there are reports that in many parts of the city these boys were still active in the early 1900s.

1845 – The *Crumlin Road Gaol* is a Grade A listed building that opened in 1845 as a replacement for the Gaol on Antrim Street in Carrickfergus. During its 151 years it housed murderers, loyalist and republican prisoners, suffragettes and politicians. The last execution which took place in the jail was that of Robert Mcgladdery in 1961.

In 1847 laws were passed that if you were unemployed you could be branded on your forehead with the letter V for vagrant. If you remained unemployed you would be made a slave and the penalty for a third offence was death. This act was later repealed in 1849. The *Vagrancy Act of 1824* had made it illegal for vagrants to be seen in public as it was believed that vagrancy was caused by extreme idleness. In 1837 an amendment was passed which allowed for vagrants to be fed and cared for in poorhouses until they could properly upkeep a job. Sailors and Deserters from the army were also branded with various letters according to their crime including BC for 'Bad character'. Human Branding was not abolished until the 1840s.

1850s There were two theatres in the Smithfield area of Belfast, *The Millgate* and *The Hibernian*. Not much is known of *The Hibernian* but *The Millgate* ran two shows daily including performances of *Julius Caesar*.

1857 – *Sincler Seamans* Presbyterian Church is built the current interior refurbishment resembles the interior of a ship.

1868 – On the 28th June the new Masonic Hall at Arthur Square is formally opened, prior to this date Belfast Masons met in several places.

1869 – The Albert Clock was completed

1883 – (ISSUU.com) On 2nd March 1883 'The Belfast Newsletter' reported that bones had been found on the junction of North Street were Messrs Foster Green and Co were cutting the foundations for their new premises. They dug deeper and found the remains of an old garrison wall. The heads were removed from the bodies and several random bones were found. The reason for the bones being buried where they were has been cause for much speculation. If the heads were removed from bodies after hanging and placed on spikes as a deterrent there is no reference to it in the histories of Belfast.

1885 – The Ulster Reform Club opened as Belfast's first gentlemen's club outside Masonic circles.

1895 – *The Grand Opera House* is opened.

2nd March 1883

I can feel my hands grow clammy, my breath coming in long slow gasps and sweat start to form on my brow. This morning's edition of the *Northern Whig* has me reaching for the whisky and it is not even eight o clock. The words on the page swim before my eyes

At the present time foundations are being built at the corner of North Street and Royal Avenue for an extensive establishment to be erected for Messers Foster Green and Co. It will, when completed, adjoin their North Street premises. When the workmen were engaged in cutting the first section of the foundations, they came across some interesting relics of old Belfast. At one place they found a number of human skulls and bones……

I knew …….

I knew my secret had been unearthed and yet I had not known where it was buried. I had not the ranking to be privy to all their secrets.

Apparently we live our lives as a tale which is told. There are times I wish I could tell the tale of my life to others and times I believe it should stay untold, buried with their secrets….and mine. Yet I do not regret my role in what was to come. My early years were very uninteresting but yet they ultimately paved the way for the path that I took.

Who am I?

I am Virgil Black born in late February in the year of our Lord 1827. My parents were farmers in County Antrim, they survived on an income which was 'cut to suit the cloth' my mother would say. Both my mother and father taught me the value of money and made sure I could cope outside of a farm living. I had never been fond of the animals but yet they were all that was known in my vicinity. My parents brought me up properly with education and religion. Three times to church on a Sunday and often weeknights we watched the preacher with a rotund countenance and ruddy complexion pontificate from the pulpit, as he warned that we would go to hell and be punished for all our evil thoughts and deeds. Drink was the way of fools and the way to the devil, but yet, he always looked like he had an alcoholic flush.

Hypocrisy is something I have learned saturates every level of our society. I see it more with my old age than I did then. At some stage I started questioning everything that I was being taught and turned against various aspects of my upbringing. Maybe I had my reasons and maybe I needed new ways to cope.

At the age of 14 I left school and gained an apprenticeship in a local business. My parents had not had me educated just to run a farm. The premises consisted of a small haberdashery and hardware store. The town was not big but the gleaming white and blue exterior of the shop could be recognised the length of the Main Street. I learnt over the next three years how to cut materials, to tailor, what to treat the material with, the value of various different fabrics and the exact amount that would be required for a dress or a suit. The owner taught me how to balance the books and to stock take. They showed me how to entice the customer with matching accessories which may also be added to the outfit. I learnt the difference between various types of plants, vegetables and berries and what tools should be used for planting. Everything I learnt about money, material and substances I learnt at this business.

When I had just passed my eighteenth birthday I was invited to a dance at the home of a local banker. Mr McAuley had been so pleased with the new suits we had tailored for him that I was included in the invitation. I had previously only entered large houses by the back door, being given the standing of a servant. On this night I entered by the front door and was announced by a butler.

It felt good!

This was also my first time at such an evening; people like me do not get invited to the homes of the upper classes. Mr. Fox the owner of the shop had me well instructed to mind my manners, how to introduce myself and under no circumstances to give an opinion on anything I knew nothing about. The high vaulted ceiling of the ballroom left me in awe. How was it possible to have so much detail in the rosewood panelling and the flowers carved into the sconces were very intricate. A fresco adorned one wall which was easily recognisable as the house and gardens. At the time I remember thinking why had they painted a picture on the wall (I had never seen a fresco before)? There were at intervals grand tables with lions feet legs surrounded by chairs I would be too afraid to sit on. It was such a contrast to the three legged stool that sat by the fire at home with the big black pot sitting beside the skillet. Never had I seen so much food.

I managed to distract my eyes from the feast and it was then I set my eyes on the girl with the flaxen coloured hair. She was staring at me with a gleam in her eye as if amused by my obvious awe in my surroundings.

I smiled at her shyly and walked toward her rather hesitantly as I was entirely unsure if my instructions for this evening included talking to the females, and I hadn't thought to ask.

Stretching out my hand I took the proffered one of hers shaking it rather too vigorously and introducing myself as Mr. Black, as I had been instructed. The flaxen beauty informed me she was called Miss McAuley. Perhaps I did not put two and two together at the time, but I did not realise she was our hosts daughter. We made polite conversation regarding the weather and how it has been unusually dry for this time of year. I remarked on the spread of food and, perhaps foolishly, on how I had never seen so much at once. She laughed at me. I am still unsure at whether this because I was too honest or because I was so obviously not of the same class. I was ultimately saved from further embarrassment by the timely arrival of Mr. Fox who directing me by the elbow escorted me none to gently away, before I could even excuse myself from her company.

'Do you know who that girl is?' he had asked with raised eyebrows and his fingers still pinching my arm. Never in the four years working for him had I seen him as flustered.

I replied 'she told me she was called Miss McAuley' as I spoke the words, I knew I had made a mistake. How was I to know that I was not permitted to speak to the host's daughter?

Mr.Fox asks 'I hope you did not say anything out of line or that may have impact on the business?'

'No', I reply softly in a suitably contrite tone, 'we only talked about the weather'.

He seemed satisfied with my answer. Realising his hand was still attached to my arm he loosened his grip and dropped his arm.

'Let us retire to the games room and I shall show you how to play some games that should keep you out of trouble!' he had said.

I knew from the minute I entered the room if my father asked what I had done tonight he was not going to be happy. In front of me through the tobacco smoke and flickering light of the oil lamps were half a dozen green felt covered tables folded out into squares. Each table surrounded by men smoking and holding hands of cards.
If I sat and watched these men I was going to hell. Mr. Fox wanted me to play, was that going to be twice the punishment? I remember thinking to myself I'd never even make it as far as hell if my father knew I was playing the 'Devil's cards'. He would kill me first.

Mr. Fox enquired if we could join the game closest to the fire.

We sat.

My knees trembled, despite the heat, as I thought of the retribution which was to come. This was my first game of 'gin'. I was not great at it to start but I did pick it up quite quickly. We then moved on to poker, which I was better at once I realised it is as much about convincing your opponents that you have a good hand even if you do not. If we had been playing for money that night I do believe I would have pocketed a fair penny.

Our host joins our company towards the end of the evening. He tells us he had to dance any more his feet would fall off.

'It's all about keeping the women happy after all', he laughs 'That daughter of mine cannot sit still, never has been able to, always ready to dance'.

The noise and chatter in the room had risen due to the occupants now having consumed copious amounts of drink. I had also partaken of a glass or two of whisky. Strong stuff and something I was also going to regret doing, no doubt. Maybe I had one too many but everything seemed blurred and I found it hard to hear. Mr McAuley asks me if I am the boy who had made his suits. I let him know that it was indeed my handiwork.

'What else do you do boy? Do you always intend in working in a shop?' he enquires.

Having not really thought about the answer to this question before, I respond, 'I am good with figures, I am able to keep all Mr. Fox's accounts and perhaps in time I may open my own business'.

He seems satisfied with the response and informs me that he has an acquaintance who would be looking new cashiers in his bank in Belfast.

I had never been outside my town and Belfast to me might as well have been a foreign country. However, the idea of a job in a city with good money intrigued me. I asked him to give me more information. When the jobs would be starting and if he thought I had enough experience. Mr. McAuley informed me that he would make an enquiry the next time he was in town and get back to me with all the details. It did not seem unusual to me that he should be helping me in this way and I was very grateful that he should think of me. My parents however would not be happy if I was to move so far away. However, if they found out I had been playing cards tonight no matter what age I am I might have to emigrate.

I did not mention the job to my parents and managed to escape the next morning despite having spent several hours in the outside privy, retching my insides out at both ends.

I do not recall how long it had taken for Mr. McAuley to return with news of the job. I remember it had been very cold out and possibly almost winter when he had returned with the 'good news'. He had entered the shop accompanied by his daughter. She had a red velvet cloak adorning her shoulders trimmed with fur. I did not think that the colour suited her it made her pale features look fragile. Green or pale blue would have suited her pallor much better. I did not pay her much attention as I was very aware of being watched by two other sets of eyes, for Mr. Fox had now entered the main shop. This was the first he was to hear that I may move to the 'big smoke'. Mr. McAuley informed us both that Mr. Coulter would be expecting me two weeks from today if I were to take up the situation. Mr. Fox appeared shocked and did not say much in front of the more distinguished gentleman, but I knew he was not happy. I could not go as far as to say sad, for he would now be a few pounds short each month without my contribution to the tailoring business. I had already determined that I would accept the offer.

In my head I had been rehearsing how I would tell my family but had not settled on any particular way. Perhaps I should just say it straight and have done. I knew they would be sad to see me leave but they had me educated for an opportunity such as this and I intended to grab it while it was offered.

On leaving the store Mr. McAuley informed me that I should call on him that evening. I should not dress for dinner as he wished to discuss further matters with me.

I had walked home that evening taking the long way across some of the neighbouring farmland. I knew I would have to inform mother and father as soon as I arrived home. They would be wondering why I would not be going to meeting that evening and what would be so important to abandon an hour with the Lord.

I walked through the back yard to the door, for in these parts everyone seemed to always use the backdoor as the front and the front door was only for the vicar. Pushing open the heavy wooden door I immediately smelt the food on the stove and to this day the smell of broth makes me slightly queasy. The heat of the stove hit me and with the flush on my face from walking I felt it redden further.

I stood in the middle of the doorway cap in hand head bowed and mumbled, 'I've been offered a job in Belfast, in a bank'. 'Jobs like this don't come along very often for people in these parts and I've told Mr. McAuley from the big house that I'll take it'.
Before they could respond I added, 'I can't go to bible class tonight I've been asked to go up to the house for a meeting with Mr. McAuley'.

There was silence for what felt like an age.

Then my father got up and shook my hand.

'Well done boy, you'll be able to keep us all soon on the wages you'll be making'. 'I don't approve of him up there in the big house though; he does not think much about God'. You would be well to avoid contact with him as much as you can or you will fall into the devil's ways'. He informed me.

In reply I told him 'I will find a church to attend as soon as I get to town. I'm sure there will be a few more to choose from there in a bigger place'. This seemed to appease him for the moment.

My mother wrung her hands on her apron and laid the plates on the table before coming around to the other side and hugging me, her tears falling in my hair.

'You've worked hard Virgil but we will miss you, sure you will be able to afford to come home and visit', she sobbed.

Not as hard as I thought it would be to tell them, I knew they were upset at the suddenness of the news but they trusted God would look after me wherever the new work took me. I found it hard to swallow the vegetable broth but I finished it with a lump of bread. Then I went and washed my face before heading out in the dark to the 'big house'.

This time I took the fastest route as it would not be sensible to try and navigate too far in the dark. Arriving at the door I rub my shoes on the back of my trousers to shine them up a bit. I remove my cap and rub my hand through my hair to make myself feel more respectable.

I announce my arrival by way of the large brass door knocker which I noticed was in the shape of a dragon. The same man answers the door as had the night of the dance. I noticed he was rather gaunt and ill looking as he greeted me.

'Good evening Mr. Black you are expected please follow me'.

He leads me down a dark corridor decorated with what appears to be red velvet wallpaper and illuminated by small oil lamps. He opens the door into what I assume to be a large living room and asks me to wait. I have time to look around me at the various oil paintings all of which appeared to portray fallen angels, demons and serpents. One depicts Adam and Eve in the Garden of Eden the serpent in between them about to devour Eve. There is a fire lit in the centre of the room and a rather large chaise placed in close proximity to it. I sat closest to the fire as I was slightly shivering possibly from both the cold and nerves. I am unsure how long I sit and I am impatient and I also get the impression that someone else is in the room even though there is no one in sight.

After what seemed like an eternity the door opens and Mr. McAuley's daughter enters the room closing the door behind her. She is dressed in a moss green silk dress the top of which is very revealing. It almost looks like the top is the corset of her under garments. Dare I say improper for a lady of such a standing. I notice that her breasts are pushed up so far with the corset that they are nearly falling out the top. For an eighteen year old she is very well developed. I feel my self redden at the sight of her. She smiles and I stand having forgotten my manners with the thoughts currently running through my head. I could feel my trousers tighten and after politely shaking her hand I wait until she sits before through necessity placing my cap on my lap.

'Are you well Mr. Black?' she asks 'I am very sorry you have not been offered refreshments'. She rises from the chaise and heads to the side of the fireplace where there is a compartment in the wall, once opened it revealed a drinks cupboard. 'What would you like to drink?'

Unsure of whether it was mannerly to refuse the drink or not I ask for whisky and hope I do not have to have more than one.

She pours herself one as well which I find very odd. Is it usual for young women to drink whisky? Then returns to the chaise where she sits rather close to me. I take my drink much too quickly in my unease and find myself coughing. It clears quickly thank goodness and I have enough wits about me to ask 'Shall Mr McAuley be along shortly?

'He has been held up momentarily I am afraid with one of my cousins from Belfast who is staying with us', she replies. 'I was curious to find out more about you after the party you did look so out of place'.

'It was the first time I had been invited to such an evening and I was nervous. Mr. Fox usually attends such functions on his own. Your father was very happy with my work and had said I may attend with Mr. Fox this time. It is not the company I am used to'. I responded.

She seemed to have moved closer to me as I could now smell her perfume, something vaguely flowery and sickeningly sweet like Rose or Lily. I was feeling very hot under the collar of my Sunday best shirt and I know if I moved I would feel a lot more uncomfortable further down. I had never sat this close to a female, as most times the local girls were chaperoned by a relative or were at church. I had of course had urges which I knew were normal. Living on a farm after all you see all sorts of mating going on with the animals from a very young age. It was however preached in church by the rotund preacher that fornication was a sin. I took that he meant any form of sexual deed outside of marriage, including relieving yourself of urges. I had been getting them a lot more recently and surely it was easier to relieve ones self than fornicate. I was feeling very uncomfortable as she moved closer and I found that her breasts were very close to my face as she lifted my hand.

'Father got me this dress especially made by his last tailor. What do you think of the material doesn't it feel nice?' She placed my hand on the material covering her breast. 'The tailor left very suddenly and I think you could make me another'. 'The corset should be tighter around my waist should it not?' She queries as she lifts my other hand and places them both now around her waist.

In a state of shock I let her place them there, watching her cleavage move up and down with what appears to be exaggerated breathing. A dragon shaped pendant hanging around her neck, takes its place between her breasts. I should have stopped her but what teenage boy thinks with his head when his privates are in full functioning mode. I should have thought her father would be very cross, and I won't get my job and I'll probably end up in jail or worse.

I let her place my hands and having not touched a woman before I feel the roundness of her buttocks as I circle her waist. It occurs to me that this material is either very thin or she does not have on under garments. When she leans in to kiss me I do not stop her. My first kiss and such soft lips. I do not notice that she has pulled us backwards and I am now lying on top of her. When her hand reaches down and rubs my cock through my trousers I like it but I panic. I sit bolt upright flustered both from the thought that I really don't know what to do, and I don't know how I have come to be in this situation. She sits up and turns my cheek around to face her saying 'its alright he will be a while' while her hands reached for my breeches she kisses me again and all common sense disappears.

She is very sure of what she is doing for having the appearance of such a fragile timid creature. My trousers are pulled down and she pulls up her skirts, to reveal that she is indeed naked underneath. White stockings are all that cover her bottom half. She tells me not to look so worried and holding my cock she guides me into her. It feels warm and I thrust into her instinctively. She continues to kiss me as I grab her buttocks and in seconds I feel myself release. I am unsure if she should enjoy our coupling or if I did it right. But I got the feeling she had done this before when she says, 'next time you'll last longer'.

A disappointment then…….

I had enjoyed it but the elation does not last long as the door opens and Mr. McAuley walks in. I struggle hastily to my feet pulling up the breaches and fastening them as he looks on. I am mortified and very, very scared. Emily as I shall call her, seems rather foolish to call her Miss. McAuley after what had just ensued, readjusts her skirts with rather too little decorum. She places herself against the chaise at one end while she reclines one leg bent on the chaise the other placed on the floor. She does not look flustered and in fact looks very self assured and calm. I on the other hand have a feeling I am about to lose the use of my sphincter muscles and defecate right there in the middle of the room.

I am going to hell!!

Mr. McAuley then speaks, 'Emily leave us. Now I shall talk with Mr. Black'. His voice had an eerily calm and calculated tone.

She picks up her skirts, winks at me and leaves the room.

He walks to the front of the fireplace and remains silent for what seems like a very long time. He doesn't rock on his heels or fidget he has the stance of a man in control and who knows exactly what he is doing.

'Virgil. We have been watching you for some time. I don't just mean through the hole in the back of the drinks cabinet but for a number of years. By 'we' I mean several gentlemen. You are of a very religious background and as I have just witnessed are very naive for an 18 year old. Religion brings with it a certain discipline and as I have just witnessed you seem lacking in self discipline. Then perhaps any man faced with the prospect of 'having' Emily probably would not decline. We have been watching you in the shop taking note of your attention to detail in your work, your ability to follow instructions and your obvious inclination to progress to have better prospects. Therefore 'we' are going to give you that opportunity. You shall start your work in the bank in Belfast in a fortnight's time. Then after a month you shall be introduced to your 'other business'. In the meantime I think you should take Emily to introduce her to your parents as you shall be marrying her before the week is out. It just isn't the done thing to have intercourse out of wedlock'.

I listen shocked and not entirely sure if I hadn't had more to drink than I thought. Surely I wasn't hearing him correctly. He still wanted me to marry Emily even when it is quite clear she had trapped me for another purpose.

'Mr. McAuley, Sir, you want me to marry Emily even when it is clear I am not her first?' I stutter.

'There is a lot you have to learn boy and the first is to not question your instructions. The best way to get ahead in this world and to stay safe is to never question. You will only know what you need to know. Emily is not my daughter to my wife but she is my daughter. She is one of us raised with the purpose of continuing 'our' work. She has a greater role to play than any of us. You will marry her and you will have children the sooner the better'.

I do not know what he is on about 'we' and 'us'? I have just been instructed not to ask questions. I do anyway.

'Who are 'we'?'

Mr McAuley replies 'All shall be revealed in a matter of time. Patience is a virtue but virtuous is something we are not. The wedding shall be on Saturday prepare yourself and tell your parents whatever you feel you need to, Emily will go along with whatever story you tell'.

I vaguely remember being shown out of the house my hat still in my hands as I feel myself twisting the material. How I got home I do not know, my mind wondering if I had dreamt everything. I enter the house. Everything is in darkness and I climb into my bed for once too deep in thought to feel the cold and damp.

In the morning I come down to breakfast, I eat my porridge before I speak.

I inform my parents that I will be moving to Belfast at the end of next week and then I inform them of the unexpected.

'I met Mr. McAuley's daughter at the dance at the 'big house' and we got on well. She likes me too and I asked her to marry me'.

I wait in the silence and then add 'this Saturday'.

My father is the first to speak.

'You are both from two different classes of people which should not matter under the eyes of God but it matters to other men. You do not have a home to go to in Belfast yet and you have not enough money to support a wife and family. Marriage is not to be entered into lightly. We want you to marry a good Christian girl who respects all you have been taught and lives by the same rules'.

I respond 'Mr. McAuley has agreed to give Emily a dowry and we are to live at his premises on Donegal Street in Belfast'. He also agreed to organise the church for the weekend and place the banns in the paper'.

Mr. McAuley had not mentioned any of this but I was presuming he would attend to both the church and banns as this was all his idea.

My mother decided to add her pennies worth and informs me I do not know her well enough, we have not courted long and how do I know it is not just a passing fancy. 'Men do get these whims' she adds.

I hate lying to them but I am too scared of Mr. McAuley to go against him and I do not want my parents to know that I had shamed them by having intercourse outside of marriage. I stand up and tell them my mind is made up before picking my hat up from the stove where I left it last night and leave them to chew over and digest what they had been told.

On Thursday morning a note arrives attached to a suit. I am to attend the Old Presbyterian Church on the Main Street at 10am on Saturday morning. I should inform my parents that there would be dinner at the 'big house' immediately after the ceremony.

On Saturday morning I get up early I had not slept anyway and there was no point in lying any longer. My last night in my own bed cut short. I go out the back to the horse tail pump and wash myself in freezing cold water and duck fat soap. I do not stand any longer than I need for there is frost on the ground and I am turning blue. My mother is up when I go back in the kitchen and making breakfast. When my father comes down we share a pot of tea and a couple of wheaten farls. Not much is said while we eat.

When the food is finished father says, 'are you sure this is what you want to do?'

'Yes', I reply even though it's not what I had foreseen myself doing at the start of last week. I leave the table and go upstairs to get dressed in my new suit. The final breakfast of a condemned man or at least that is how I felt.

The church was empty save a few locals my mother had told who had obviously just popped in for a nosey. The rotund vicar with the alcoholic glow was nowhere in site and had been replaced by a tall slim man with a face resembling a skeleton and a beak nose. In that moment he resembled the grim reaper or what I imagined the reaper would look like.

Emily arrived, the ceremony went off with no hitches and after signing the register we travelled in a horse and carriage up to the house. I suppose most weddings are much the same and therefore I shall not go into details. Only that I should add my parents felt and looked very awkward sitting at the twelve foot dining table along with the McAuley family. I also felt uneasy. Not as much from the company but because I had no idea what was now expected of me.

My parents left just after dark and were escorted home in the horse and carriage. I am sure that would be some piece of gossip to share when I am gone.

They left and I was informed that the man of the house and Emily were waiting on me in the same room that I had 'sinned' in the previous week. The fire was roaring in the grate and both father and daughter where sitting at ease on the wing back seats on either side of the fire. Two other men I had not seen before sat on the chaise. Mr. McAuley got up to poke the fire and I noticed that he left the poker in the flames as he turned around.

'Welcome to the family, Virgil. I am sure we no longer need to be on formal terms in private please call me Samuel. These are two of my closest acquaintances Mr. Sinclair and Mr. Lanyon. There is one more task that we must undertake to make sure you are now entirely one of 'us' and that there shall be no mistaking your loyalty to the order. Could you please roll up your sleeve on your left arm'. Not having any notion on why I was being told to do so I roll up the sleeve. When I look up Samuel has removed what I thought was a poker from the flames. Now glowing red I see it resembles more of a branding iron with the same shape of the dragon which had appeared on their door knocker. I fear what I now know will happen, sweat beading on my brow and running down my back I turn to move back only to be held in place by the arms of the other two men. My arm facing towards the heat I barely hear the words 'welcome to the order of the red dragon' as the searing pain makes everything turn black.

The next morning I am wakened by the sound of curtains. I am very well aware of the pain in my left arm and I feel nauseous. I open my eyes to unfamiliar surroundings and the awareness that my clothes have now been removed. I am lying in a very ornate four poster bed with red velvet trimmings. There is an Egyptian style panelling which the reflection in the mirror at the foot of the bed shows to be crowned with the all Seeing Eye. Very unusual markings. I look at my arm and view the blistering red stain. The scarification is that of a red dragon and the words 'Mit blud und gehorsam' (with blood and obedience).

Emily is standing at the side of the bed 'You can make the wedding night up to me later', she chides as she throws herself down on the bed beside me. That is the furthest thing from my mind right now. I notice that her left arm also has the dragon branding, it is faded with age but an additional one underneath is new that of a large V. What have I got myself in to?

We moved to Belfast in January of 1845 taking up residence in Donegal Street, just a stones throw from the Bank and in the same quarters as Samuel. I started work in the bank and got paid almost twice what I would have in the shop. We did not pay for our accommodation so on occasion I was able to send money home to my parents. It must have been around February time that Emily informed me she was pregnant. We had since the wedding become close as it should be in a marriage and I was delighted with the news.

The baby arrived on 5th September and I was delighted that she had given birth to a son. Emily was not just happy she also seemed relieved. At the time I thought nothing of this but I was to find out a few years later why she was so happy we had a son.

My work for the order had been not too taxing as I had thought. I had been taken blindfolded to various homes where I had not met the man of the house. On entering the establishments I had been taken straight to the ladies of the house. I was expected to measure and choose fabrics to make new corsets and under garments for them. On occasion I was asked to make collars with leads attached and on one occasion to fashion a corset out of leather with room for the breasts to poke through. These women presented themselves to me in the nude and only having the experience with Emily I was entirely unsure how to carry on with my task while presented with so many delightful figures. They did not seem to notice my anxiety and nerves and I carried on as best I could under the circumstances. They seemed pleased with my work and I did not question any of my orders.

My life continued in a routine and I was happy with my family and my work. Until 1847 when there was a national catastrophe. There were widespread problems with the crops and farmers had lost nearly all their potato crops. Many country people in Ireland survived on potatoes and the loss of their staple diet meant that a lot of people were starving. The British government did not do anything to help and pretty much washed their hands of the starving in Ireland. Many moved from the countryside to the towns and brought with them a whole new set of problems. The overcrowding and insanitary condition caused by the influx of bodies brought with it a fever epidemic, in the form of cholera. 'The Belfast Protestant Journal' wrote they *could hardly believe that such a state of things prevailed in a place so enlightened as Belfast'*[1]. The epidemic was at its worst in Belfast[2] with one in every seven people succumbing to the fever. *Donegal Street* where we lived was one of the most affluent areas in town but at the foot of the street near the *Linen Hall* was one of Belfast's most deprived areas know as the 'Half Bap'. Here people lived some eight or more people to a house and there were houses backing on to each other with open sewers. It is also said that in the shebeens off *York Street*[3] that people were so hungry they ate rats alive.

Emily as part of her work for the 'Red Dragon' was often sent to the poorhouse of *Clifton Street* to see if there were any persons which she could recruit. I was not informed what sort of person they looked for and often wondered why they sent a

---

[1] Quote from 'The Hidden Famine: Hunger, Poverty and Sectarianism in Belfast 1840-50'. It is often said that the Irish famine was one of the biggest acts of genocide ever recorded. Professors Charles Rice and Francis Boyle believed, *the policies pursued by the British Government from 1845-1850 in Ireland constituted genocide'.*
George E Pataki governor of New York State petitioned to have the Irish Famine taught alongside the Holocaust. *History teaches us the great Irish hunger was not the result of a massive failure of the Irish potato crop but rather the result of a deliberate campaign by the British to deny the Irish people the food that they need to survive.*
[2] May 1847 Belfast was in the middle of a fever epidemic.
[3] ISSUU.com

female. She had left the boy who we called Lucas with me often on Saturday afternoons while she went about her business. She had not been attending as often due to the fever. On 15th January 1847 she returned as usual complaining of a headache. I fetched her some water and smelling salts and she retired to bed. That night as I was retiring I noticed she was sweating and seemed somewhat delirious. I called for a local physician who after checking her over informed me she had the fever. The symptoms would get worse over the next few days and maybe weeks but I should expect the worse as cases had increased rapidly over the last few days. Extra sheds had been opened at the poorhouse and they had reopened the old cholera hospital to cope with the number of cases. I was informed that there was no point in sending Lucas away to the country as we were both probably infected already.

Emily's condition continued to decline along with the general population of Belfast[4] the papers reported daily that the number of deaths were in there hundreds. Funerals were forgotten along with other sanctities of death. The new graveyard at *Clifton Street* was burying over a hundred bodies a week and at the height of the fever. Up to five bodies were placed in coffins which were no more than boxes. The situation was so bad that the old cholera graveyard was opened as a mass grave on the *Antrim Road* and due to lack of space bodies were buried between the walls and the road.

Emily deteriorated and became weaker coughing up blood and no longer had any energy. In the meantime Lucas also came down with the fever. I found it hard to cope with them both ill in the house. I had seemed to have survived any symptoms so far. Perhaps it was the country up bringing. I made sure everything was boiled in hot water and cleaned with the water from inside. All linens were also to be cleaned with the inside water and not from the outside pump. Both Emily and the boy did not last long after Lucas had presented with symptoms. Due to the number of deaths a ceremony seemed highly unlikely and I informed Emily's father of the deaths and asked his advice.

---

[4] Due to the overcrowding in Belfast, the changing circumstances in the country and rapidly increasing population of the town. The number of famine and fever deaths in Belfast is unknown.

Mr. McAuley seemed genuinely grieved at the loss of his daughter. He informed me that it would not be possible to have a ceremony.

'We had expected Emily to live a lot longer and provide you with a lot of daughters. At least until you had moved up the ranks of 'the order' and were privy to a few more of our secrets. The fact of the matter is Emily does not exist on paper, neither her birth your marriage or that of the birth of your child are recorded anywhere. We shall take care of her body and that of the child'.

'What shall you do with them?' I asked not caring if I was disobeying orders.

This once he answered my question 'We shall leave them with the other bodies at the gate of the cemetery to be buried in a mass grave'.

I could not bare the thought of them being in an unmarked grave and forgotten as if they had never existed. I asked him to wait until tomorrow and to give me a chance to say good bye. I had not presented with symptoms thus far, one more night would not hurt.

Despite Emily's weight loss over the passed weeks she was still heavy and would have been noticeable to move in the dark. I therefore resigned myself to the fact that I would have to live by her father's wishes. The child however was small and looked so fragile as he lay still in his cot. I wrapped him in one of Emily's red velvet cloaks and left the house. The only thing I could think of was to leave him at the church. I placed him on the doorstep and prayed for the first time in two years that God would forgive me.[5]

I let Samuel take care of Emily's body he did not ask where the body of the child had gone and I did not volunteer the information. We carried on as if nothing had ever happened and as if they had never existed. My days were filled with work at the bank and I filled my evenings with tailoring and the occasional trip to the

---

[5] On 27th February 1847 the body of an unknown child thought to be around two years old was found on the doorstep of a church. ISSUU.com

theatre at *Smithfield*. Drawing also seemed to free my mind, letting the strokes on the paper absorb some of what is in my head.

In September of the same year the fever and famine were at their worst in Antrim and both my parents succumbed. I was not with them in the end and had not seen them since the previous summer. All I had left was a letter from the rotund minister to say they had passed on and had been buried at the local graveyard. He added; could you please forward the cost of the funeral.

In the years that followed I worked as much as I could filling my empty hours with theatres and alcohol. I found I had grown to like the taste. Maybe that was a lie. I never liked the taste except maybe of whisky. I drank it none the less and it numbed any feelings I had for a time. In my sober hours I was introduced to 'The Order of the Red Dragon' a little at a time.

It resembled a pyramid system where you knew very few members and those at the bottom of the pyramid the proletariat of the order knew the least of all. Each level had its own benefits and individual tastes. The top level, I knew very little about other than it consisted of only twelve members. If you managed to make it that far you either had very good credentials or you had a very sadistic view on life.

The bottom level member is where I found myself in 1848 having tailored several dozen outfits in the period since I arrived in Belfast. I knew nothing about the running of meetings as I had up until now not been invited to attend. On the death of my wife and child I received my first invitation. All meetings were held in various locations around the city or outskirts of town and were top secret events. No one outside the order knew about them and members only found out their destination on arrival.

My first meeting was in the centre of town. I was collected in a carriage and instructed to wear formal wear with a red rose in the left pocket of the jacket. On arrival I was escorted into a very ornate house almost regal in nature such was the opulence of the décor. The ballroom was decorated with the customary red velvet trimmings hanging from the sconces on the ceiling. The candelabras descended from the centre of rose shaped carvings hanging at intervals throughout the room. The candles flickered to provide an almost supernatural feel to the room. At the top of the room where what appeared to be two thrones both gold gilded with purple fabric seats. In each seat sat a man dressed in a mask and suit. The room itself was not laid out for dancing but with several games tables and copious amounts of food and alcohol.

The men rose to their feet both tapping what appeared to be large spectres on the floor. The head of each sceptre was that of a brass dragon.

'Welcome brothers', said the man on the left. 'We welcome tonight some new members to our order and hope that they shall be made feel at home. You will recognise them only from the rose in their pocket. You are reminded to not reveal anything about yourselves to any other members and that anything that happens within these walls should be taken with you to the grave. The penalty for disobeying these rules shall be carried on the edge of a sword'.

Up until now I still knew very little about 'the dragons' and so far it appeared to be just a group of men gathering for cards and drinks.

However, as the men returned to their thrones, the doors at either side of the room opened and in walked ten women dressed in corsets and petticoats. All in various different colours and styles I recognised the ones which I had designed. The women stood at the side of the card tables while we played. The drinking started to get out of hand and one of the men grabbed one of the women and pulled her onto his lap. He pulled up her petticoats and revealed her backside. Turning her around to face the table petticoats around her waist, he slapped her, the buttocks turning pink with the force. Shocked I said nothing. I could not. We had been warned. He then removed his jacket placing it neatly on the back of his chair. He removed his belt and proceeded to use it to hit her with gently at first but he became more savage in his strokes. While this happened the woman said nothing. She obeyed. I could say the glint in her eyes as she fought back the tears.

'Do you like this whore?' he spat as he continued to wield his leather lash, purple welts already beginning to form on her ass and legs. He did not stop until he drew blood and she did not so much as murmur a sound.

When he finished he commanded that she turn around and undoing his trousers he pushed her head down and demanded that she suck on him.

I had never witnessed anything of this nature and was at once both scared and intrigued. The savage nature of the treatment and the voyeuristic nature of the actions had me watching in awe.

He pushed her head onto him so that she was barely able to breathe and demanded that she look into his eyes. He did not release her until she started to turn purple from lack of air. Then he asked if anyone else wanted a piece of his 'whore'.

She did as she was commanded as he ripped the bodice top from her shoulders and revealed her breasts. Another gentleman moved from the other side of the table. He grabbed her so she was standing her buttocks in the air facing him as she was almost asphyxiating on the other man's cock. He too undid his trousers and demanding she hold her buttocks apart he slammed himself into her hard. One man in her mouth the other in her ass the cochineal eye make up she was wearing ran down her face as she struggled to compose herself and not cry with the pain, blue streaks staining her face. Both men seemed to take a great deal of pleasure out of causing her pain. I continued to watch but I did not join in. I did notice that similar such acts were occurring with the other women in the room, some of them not as quiet as they were being told to scream. It was obvious that in many cases this screams were real. Yet they obeyed their masters. They were our slaves to be done with as we please 'mit blud und gehorsam'. Towards the end of the evening I noticed the men had left the women in various states of consciousness and undress. They were bruised and beaten and a couple looked lucky to be alive.

Now I knew why Emily was always looking for recruits at the poorhouse. At least she had the fortunate chance to die as she did for this would have been a cruel fate. Glad also that we had no daughters for no daughter of mine would have been taking part in such abhorrent activities. Could I have stopped it though? I am no one and they are many. I realised there would be no escaping this life and the only way out was death. Obeying would be the only way to live.

Obey I did.

I made new clothes, there were many over the years. I moved up several levels in the order. Each level showing me a new level of female degradation and treatment not even fit for animals. The females were slaves and those who managed to survive the first few tiers of the perverted hierarchy met with different sets of rules.

The women in the first tier I learnt were free to come and go as they pleased during the day. They were not likely to stray far with various bruises and cuts. They mostly came back and if they didn't they were taken care of by others. These women dressed like ladies their hair immaculate their make up pristine, the arsenic filled face creams making them less than at full health, but then they were more amiable. The belladonna they used for tinting their faces and dilating their pupils causing hallucinations and preventing them feeling the full force of their injuries. Often they were kept with drink and to get their next fix they did as they were asked. These women had mostly been obtained from the poorhouse and were listed as vagrants. They did not obtain the branding of the order but had already been branded with the 'V' for vagrant in prison or elsewhere. No one would notice they were missing.

These women were beaten and abused for the pleasure of the largest level of the order and their sadistic pleasures. Sadists at heart they often did not move above this level of perversity.

The second level was slightly different. The women were still slaves but they were dressed differently. The leather collars I had made adorned their necks like dogs. They wore nothing but the leather corsets with the open breast. Their bottom halves and breast exposed for instant access.

They served the food to the men at the table with dignity. The men carried on conversations and acted as if this was just like a normal feast. The difference was the women were dessert, shared between the guests so they could all have a piece of them. Like animals they were whipped, chained, spat on and rode. Indeed in some cases forced to wear saddles and tails in their anuses to resemble ponies. The men used every part of them and in some cases all parts at once. Very often the pain and screams of these women could have been heard miles away. These meetings were held out in the countryside away from prying ears. I must admit at times these deeds turned me on and on occasion I let them suck on my cock. Every man needs a release. But I never beat them or injured them in any way.

The third level was different again.

These women were told what to do including what they could eat, when they could eat, how much sleep they could have and how they should stand or walk. The slept naked hand cuffed to beds. Each slave had a room of their own and each guest could have a slave. How do I know what others did? I asked the slaves as I was inclined to attend to one on each occasion I attended these meetings.

They were not given names and a lot of them only knew other women were there due to the screams and activities in the night. The woman I got most information out of was called Donna, I asked her real name. She was a tall brunette with the letter F burnt into her cheek from being caught creating a menace of herself in public, the F was for fray. She had met two gentlemen one night at a bar in Bristol and offered them her services. Never having done this before and being a bit naïve she took them to her home. She presumed they had used chloroform to knock her out. The next thing she new she was waking up in chains here in this building. She thought she was in Ireland because of the accents of the men.

They had washed her and trimmed her hair all while she was unconscious. Then she had wakened chained by her right hand lying in this four poster bed. The same set of Egyptian hieroglyphs adorned the bed as had the one on my wedding night.

She said they unchained her twice a day to let her wash and go to the bathroom, feeding her just enough to keep her curves to please the men. The men came in once a day, more often from the upper level just looking some quick fun. They often unchained her from the bed then shackled her to the post in the middle of the room. Facing the post hands bound legs stretched apart they spanked her then inserted objects into her. They said they were training her ass to take a man. Each time the objects were bigger stretching her further, opening her so she could be used and abused. Each time it hurt a little less but it still felt unnatural.

In time they would take her and use her as a group all together abusing and sodomising her for their own satisfaction. By the time I got to this level of the order I had learnt this was indeed called 'sadism'. How they ever thought I country lad like myself would ever fit in and enjoy this way of life and hedonism I do not know. It was like being in Sodom and Gomorrah.

I had read various works by the 'Marquis de Sade' he had such a moralistic way of justifying his cruel acts. The book *Justine* could almost have been a diary of events which I had witnessed over the years. Like Justine many of the girls had fallen into bad company and disrepute because they had turned from degrading themselves. They had trusted in the wrong people in society and been chosen to live this life whether they wanted it or not. Very few of the girls and women enjoyed this way of life. It is frightening that the occasional woman gets off on the pain that is delivered onto them. They almost beg for more. I am unsure if they enjoy the pain itself or if the pain makes them feel alive. In this way of life they almost certainly face death.

I also used Donna for sex I never enjoyed it but I found her attractive. She would never be my wife but she was there for that purpose. If I had not used her both of us may have found that we did not like the punishments that would be bestowed on us by the 'Order of the Red Dragons'. Since my earlier years I had found I neglected God and was no longer the optimist that I had been as a boy. My one lack of judgement had turned me to a life of sin and debauchery and meant I was living my life as a puppet of a well oiled machine. The strings being pulled and I followed their direction.

Since my first years in the order I had known two men to defy the upper order. There may have been more but they defied orders in public in a meeting. They were not disciplined for killing one of the women for that seemed to be accepted as a residual expenditure. They chose to question the orders and defy the rules of secrecy. One of the gentlemen having boasted in public that he had taken these women whenever he wanted in secret places throughout the country.

He had arrived at a gathering as usual and the throne was set at the head of the room as was the norm. The man on the right hand side this time arose almost as if he was the right hand of God. Calling the man by name as was not allowed he summoned him to the throne. He ordered him to kneel and bend his head.

'What are the rules of this order?' he asked.

The man replied 'to ask no questions and to follow orders. Tell no one else of the existence of this group'.

There was no reply, a sword was drawn and in one swift slice the man's head left his body landing with a thud on the floor. Blood shot from what was left of the man's neck covering those closest.

'Must I remind you that punishment is delivered at the edge of a sword?' the man on the right hand side said before returning to his seat.

This one incident was enough to show me I did not want to cross anyone. I followed all orders and passed myself as best I could without damaging any of the women.

Donna and I agreed it was best to follow orders and so what was expected. Even it was to go through the motions. You never knew who was looking through keyholes.

I studied myself in the looking glass before leaving the house that evening. No longer a skinny lad of eighteen, at thirty two years old I had started to fill out mostly from too much food and alcohol. My once long black hair had started to grey in places and all that resembled what was once a care free lad were my eyes. Still as blue as they had been ten years ago but with a new scar just below my left eye tiny unless you were looking for it. I had made an effort this evening and was wearing my best suit with an ivory silk cravat. This suit I had not made myself. I did not get much time for that while making corsets and collars. I had made an effort none the less and was determined that I was going to stop drinking as much. The alcohol did numb my thoughts of what had happened since I left the countryside. Only when I was drunk did my feelings disappear. I could not think of my dead wife, my parents, my son or the habitual slaughter, debauchery sodomy and incest which my life had become.

Ever since that first night in Mr. McAuley's house I had been fascinated with cards. There are of course many types your everyday calling card just to let your society friends know you have called or are 'in town', the cards we receive for dances or small informal gatherings, invitations to births deaths and marriages and the new Christmas cards of which we can create our own designs. These everyday trivialities do not interest me..... I have always been fascinated with the 'devils cards'. Again there are variant types your average deck made up of 52 cards including hearts, clubs, spades and diamonds. These are most common in the gentlemen's clubs; whist and black jack among the many games on which you can gamble if the notion takes you.

These everyday cards are derived from the real 'devil's cards' if that is what you dare to call them. The Tarot is the name by which they are most commonly known. Tarot cards can be traced to the fifteenth century although they have been about for centuries it is thought as far back as ancient Egypt. They re-emerged not long into the eighteenth century in France. Mystical cards associated with divination and the occult. They contain many artistic depictions 78 in total in the deck we use now. The tarot contains four suites just like the other card sets; cups, pentacles, wands and swords. Each suite is made up of ten pip cards and four higher cards. There are also an additional 21 trump cards together with the fool making up a 'major arcana'. The other 14 cards are the 'minor arcana'. Each card has its own often hand painted pictograph and in mystic readings whatever cards you are dealt will show a revelation.

The cards are not found or read in polite society unless by a fortune teller or mystic at a fair. Then they are looked upon as a joke a form of entertainment. There are not taken seriously and that is a mistake. I have witnessed what they can show and I do not believe they should be taken lightly. I have always been open to ideas, suggestion some may say or perhaps easily influenced. They are wrong. Just because they do not understand the unknown does not mean it does not exist. Consider the blind masses that place their faith in a Christ they cannot see. They would tell you that just because you cannot see him does not mean he is not there. I argue the same point with the readings of tarot. Just because we do not fully understand something does not mean the symbolism and divination do no contain truth or premonitions.

At this time I was still single I had been invited to a small informal gathering at the home of a middle aged spinster friend. These informal gatherings were for the purpose of Tarot readings among other incendiary activities provided by 'the order'.

The evening must have been chilly not because I remember the weather but because she arrived in a black cloak. From my location in the entrance to the upper lounge I saw her enter the hallway. The first thing I noticed when she removed the hood was her hair. Bright red curls escaped to frame a pixie like face with bright blue eyes that seemed to take in everything in the surroundings. A sceptic might say she was checking out the exits. A dark moss green corset topped dress trimmed with lace displayed a curvy figure not plump but womanly in all the right places. She walked across the chequered black and white floor to stand in the middle of the stairway her countenance framed by the two marble pillars on either side of the stairs. I had a prime view from the upper banister as she ascended the stairs.

I had been unsure which activities I should partake of this evening. However, as she walked towards the table her red hair dancing like flames in the candlelight. I made the impromptu decision that the Tarot would be a good start. I followed her and pulled out a seat for her as I introduced myself as Mr. Black. She responded that she was glad to make my acquaintance and that she was Miss Rose. Volunteering that her parents must have been avid botanists as her first name was Lily.

I picked up on the fact that she had said 'her parents must have been' implying that she either did not know them or they had died when she was young. Either that or she was another 'Red Dragon' initiate who had a story for when in public gatherings. That would be something to discuss later if I felt I wasn't prying. I had not had a reading in some time but was in no rush to have my turn. The cards had the solitary position in the middle of the red velvet table covering, both tempting and forbidden. Perhaps I have a lust for things which I should not have.

The Oil lamp flickered at the centre of the table as Miss Rose was the first to have her cards read a Celtic cross reading made up of five cards. This consisted of The Priestess, The lovers, The Devil, The moon and The Eight of Swords.

'The High Priestess' is a card associated with the higher arcana of cards. This card depicts a solitary female figure who sits upright between two pillars. One of the pillars is white the other black symbolising opposites. This could be male or female, day or night, conscious or unconscious. She appears innocent of all that surrounds her yet her posture shows a position of knowledge and a sign of inner control. The presence of the crescent moon shows promise and potential but is also influential as many things can be seen secretively and are therefore just as influential as what we can see plainly. If this card appears in a reading it is unlikely you will know what is happening until it happens. 'The High Priestess' must be approached with patience for it is likely that she sees more clearly in a dream state. A spiritual card with sexual overtones may mean you become more physically attractive to others; you should however rely on your intuition and dreams. Take the path less obvious to avoid this confrontation and listen to your instincts.

'The Lovers' card is also a member of the higher arcana. It shows a young man dressed in blue standing between two women. If cupid fires his arrow at the heart of the young man the first woman he sees will inflame his passions. To choose one is to sacrifice the other. This card is about commitment the idea of considering all the options open to us and there potential ramifications. It does not necessarily mean a choice between two partners. It could be anything in your life that requires a big decision. There is a struggle for inner wisdom and the chance that following our heart will bring love to the centre of your life.

Physical love may become an obsession weakening the power to choose wisely. You may not be able to see all transformations and judgement may be blinded. In the present this card can represent a relationship which has the power to change each others lives. A card linked to clandestine meetings and all consuming passions conflicts will arise.

The evening passed peacefully and I did try to stay off the whisky so that I could get acquainted better with Miss. Rose. I do not think that any woman since Emily had me actually wanting to get to know them. Then again there are the other factors at play, including 'the order'. Perhaps I did no want them to infest anyone else's life.

I did not ask but I reckoned that she was about 22 years of age perhaps older. She informed me that she had only recently been able to venture out into society as she had been nursing an elderly friend. She did not volunteer any more details and I did not ask.

I did ask her if she was married, due to her evening gloves I could not see her ring finger. She said that in some ways she was and others she was not, but that she was promised to another. I found it odd that she talked in riddles. She appeared to be older than her years, an 'old soul' my mother would have called her.

'Are you engaged to be married then?' I asked. She replied that she was promised to the Lord and only he could decide her future. I found this extremely contrary to her actions this evening and the fact that she was playing cards and having her Tarot read.

'Mr. Black we should always live today as it is our last. *Value not ourselves in the blossom of youth. For while you are in your blossoming years ye are but ripening for the grave*'.[6]

'Surely madam you are not twenty two years old and you have a lifetime ahead of you if you are spared accident or illness. Why be so pessimistic? You have time on your side'.

'Mr. Black you do wear such an unusual pendant at your neck......perhaps you should know better than to talk of a future. When you should know that none of us are guaranteed tomorrow, especially not in social circles such as these'.

---

[6] 'The Four Fold State, p260.

Now I knew why she had not known her parents. Now I knew that she was one of them, the women who would get used and thrown out with the rubbish. She was different though. She still had an innocence about her that did not come with being used by men. She was as Emily had appeared to me the first night we had met. Yet I could sense she was not as forward. She appeared to have the knowledge but not the experience. Just like the 'High Priestess' appearing in her reading.

After some thought I responded to her statement, 'surely life is as we make it. I for one am following the life paved for me by one simple error of judgement. We reap what we sow, surely it is best to follow instructions or paths we are lead to than to walk off the beaten track and into marshy fields where we shall surely be swallowed by the earth and drown'.

'Some of us, sir, have been born and bred for a purpose we have never had the choice. Granted we have been educated and versed as ladies but to think for ourselves would be a grave sin. To follow instructions we limit our pain. We follow but one path not many. There shall not be endless pain and suffering. Like the sheep who have gone astray. There is but one throne and one end. The Lord does tell us to drink of the blood and we shall be near him. William Blake most eloquently puts it *till she who burns with youth, and knows no fixed lot, is bound in spells of law to one she loathes and must she drag the chain of life in weary lust.* This short period of time when I shall be able to socialise shall be my life for I am bound by a blood oath to follow the laws of others'.

I am entirely unsure if I am following her correctly. The riddles she speaks in I know are for the benefit of others who may be listening. I gather than she is informing me that like Emily she has been born with the sole purpose of servicing the order, both literally and figuratively but that she has followed and been obedient and that her pain shall be limited. I am intrigued. I do however fear she is telling me more than she should. The purposes of the levels in the order are to protect us each individually from other secrets. Lesser initiates are only told what they need to know. I fear I am being privy to something I should not know. Yet they never tell us something we should not know. I have a feeling my life is about to be turned inside out, if that is even possible.

I excuse myself from the company and decide to call it a night. I am not ready to join the higher order. The whole business as abhorrent to me and I find I am in need of air.
A brisk walk home straight down *Hercules Place* and across to *Donegal Street* should clear my head enough for sleep.

The next morning I am still restless I sit at the fireside a coffee pot to my right while I read my newspaper. It is the weekend and I have nothing else to encroach on my time. I cannot settle and to make matters worse there is an infernal scratching noise coming from the direction of the chimney next door. It sounds like they have a 'sooty boy' in cleaning it out. Some of my neighbours still employed the practice of using boys to clean their chimneys even though it had been illegal for a while now. My neighbour just happened to be a member of the order. I had met him on occasion and because of the rules we never mentioned that we had met outside our normal neighbourly pleasantries.

Despite the odd disruption of my routine for meetings I am stubborn and set in my ways. Some may say a grumpy old man despite my age. I enjoy doing things when I want and as I planned and I hate interruption. It takes a lot for me to vary my routine. This morning with the added thoughts in my head about Miss Rose I am agitated and the constant thumping through the back of the adjoining chimney is starting to irk me.

I hear the scream through the wall.

It is quite clearly a child in pain. I can stand it no longer. I head next door both out of annoyance, and curiosity as to what has just happened. Plus despite my nocturnal activities I cannot bear to know someone is in pain.

I had never entered the house of my neighbour prior to this event and we had been neighbours nearly eight years now. They had moved in shortly after the death of

43

Emily and the child. I kept myself to myself as I found it easiest to not answer even the most innocent of questions regarding my hobbies and other social pleasantries. I was let into the house which on first appearance appeared to be a mirror image of my own dwelling. The man was obviously not expecting guests as I could hear him shouting at the lad.

On entering the room I found the boy on the floor at the foot of the fire, the flames still roaring up the chimney. I could see the look in the man's eyes and knew he had taken an obscene delight in sending the boy up to clean the chimney of a lit fire. The boy was badly blistered and burnt already and in much pain. I asked where the sweep was and why the boy was here unattended. Normally these boys would be accompanied by an adult male. The response from my neighbour was that he had needed the sweeping done in an emergency and had grabbed the nearest poor boy he could find and offered him money. Being a cynic, what information I gleaned from those few sentences was that he had picked a boy too poor to refuse money to clean a chimney with a roaring fire as he got a perverse pleasure out of watching pain in others. The boy looked to be in a bad state and I feared he would not last long.

I turned to leave, in hindsight wishing I had not moved from my paper as the sight distressed me and I could not reprimand this man for his actions. Least said soon as mended my mother would have said, sinful curiosity is natural but we cannot unsee what has been witnessed. At the thought of my mother a verse from Genesis chapter three verse six enters my head, *we seek after knowledge rather than holiness, and study most to know the things which are least edifying, our world and roving fancies need a bridle to curb them.* Indeed Mr Fox's words from that first evening at Samuel's house also enter my head. I do believe he had taught me a valuable lesson. Do not say anything about any subject of which you do not understand. The behaviour of these men I do not think I would ever fully fathom.

I do not excuse myself from the room, I should not have been there to begin with and in regards to another member of 'the order' curiosity really would kill the cat. I just pulled the door behind me and entered the hallway.

There standing in front of me dressed in maid's clothes was Miss. Rose.

I am shocked.

What exactly is she doing in the house next door? I had never set eyes on her before last night.

Our eyes meet and I see fear in hers. She shakes her head as if she is instructing me to not talk to her. I nod my head taking one last look at her in the different attire and leave.

I return to my now cold coffee and my paper. The words remain unseen as I look but do not see. My head is now filled with more questions than I woke with and I am sure I should not be thinking of her at all. I cannot get her out of my mind.

I pace up and down the floor looking out the window, staring at the street not thinking anything in particular. My mind is full but yet it is empty.

How could she live next door and I had never seen her?

I must ask her even though I know I shouldn't.

Barely eating any food I spend the rest of the day planning how I might get to talk to her again. I get dressed as if to go out on the town and wait to see if she is going socialising again this evening. A little after eight o'clock I hear the door slam next door and check out the window. She is heading out of the house. I head straight to my front door quickly grabbing my coat and hat. I pull the door over silently before checking in which direction she is heading and following at a safe distance until I am sure she is alone.

She stops just under the street lights at *Castle Street* and I tap her on the shoulder. She is startled and quite rightly so as this is not a safe place at night. *Castle Street* is where the public hangings take place and have a grim feel during the day and even to a man who has watched many inhumane activities this place is rather overpowering at night.

'Miss Rose?' I speak as if I am unsure it is her in the flickering gas light.

'Yes Mr Black. Twice in one day this is a surprise. Where are you heading to this evening?'

I reply, 'I am unsure. I had thought I may venture to a show at *The Hibernian* at Smithfield I hear their version of *Julius Caesar* is very good. If you are not expected elsewhere would you care to join me?'

I am surprised when she agrees.

'I have only been out of the house a number of times Mr Black and all at night. I am unsure of my bearings. I thought I would just walk and see where my feet took me. I have never been to the theatre, although I have read about *The Garrick* in London and the many fine actors that take to the stage. I have also read *Julius Caesar* so perhaps seeing it on stage would be a very good distraction for the evening'.

We crossed the quarter mile in relative silence, all that could be heard was the odd sound of a drunk shouting and our feet on the cobbles, echoing in the darkness. On crossing the street to the theatre I volunteered that 'the show is supposed to be very good. There have been performances twice daily and the acting is reported to be world class'. I did not mention that I had already seen it twice while trying to occupy my time. It was a way of distracting me from the alcohol. I paid for the tickets and we took our places in the stalls. The show had already started when we arrived.

Miss Rose seemed to take in the whole surroundings as if she was internalising every little detail of the room and architecture and the people that were attending.

The show was fairly good and there was very little heckling from the audience. Indeed audiences seemed to be a lot more civilised these days. There have been shows were the audience even threw rotten fruit and vegetables at the performers if the show was terrible. She did not move the entire performance and was fully engrossed in the story right up until the curtain. I on the other hand spent most of the show looking at her out of the side of my left eye. Taking in the way her face looked as she concentrated and internalised the acting.

When the actors have left the stage we leave the auditorium with the rest of our company. I can tell she is still taking in everything around her as if she is seeing the world for the first time.

'Did you enjoy the performance?' I ask. I knew already that she had in her own way enjoyed it, not in a way that she would be overly excited, but in her own way she had liked every minute.

'Yes, Mr Black I enjoyed the experience. It is such a change to see a play in action rather than on a page. It always sticks with me that he died by so many blades. Is it not ironic that we shall probably do the same? I have always preferred *Hamlet* to *Julius Caesar*, like Ophelia I should rather go mad and drown than be bled to death'.

'Should you go straight back to your residence now or shall we get a drink and a quick bite to eat?' I ask.

'The nights are my own Mr. Black, indeed let us get some sustenance for I have not eaten much today due to the aftermath of the incident this morning'.

I do not tell her I have had nothing either, because I had been thinking about you and not the boy.

'There is a small pub of sorts around the corner *Kelly's Cellars* it is popular and we shall not be out of place at this time'.

47

It is nearly pitch dark now save for the illumination of a few street lights. The cobbles of the street are uneven. I can tell it is not as easy for a lady to walk in satin shoes with the tiny heel as she is stumbling slightly. I offer her my arm for support and we walk the short distance in companionable silence.

After a pork pie each and a glass of cider it was easier to talk. I had not had a drink in some months now and the fermented apple juice was going to my head a little too quickly. I asked her how long she had been living next door. I honestly didn't think she could have been there for the eight years without having left the house before now.

'I have been at the house of my master in *Donegal Street* since I was eighteen which is five years now, prior to that I lived at a house in the country. I was taught how to read and write like a lady and educated properly. I was also instructed in the ways of 'the dragons' from the age of sixteen. They branded me with a dragon and the words *electi rosa* which I have learnt means the 'chosen rose'. I have been taught what happens in each tier of command and how I will be treated if I stray from my path. My fate has been chosen for me. At my current residence I am treated as a slave when instructed I clean the house, or indulge my master's whims by wearing revealing clothes so that he may relieve himself with some visual stimulation. He is not allowed to touch me as he would with the other women. I am considered pure and must stay like that until it is my time to meet with our Lord'.

'Why are you giving me so much information? Surely it is against the rules to divulge this to me as I am only a mid level member. I should not be told what I do not already know'.

'You will be told more than I am telling you and soon. Samuel has stated to my master that there is now room for an upper level confidant and he has chosen you. They will vote on the decision later this week. If they choose you, you must accept if you do not there will be dire consequences. Remember once you know details, they cannot let you refuse to abide by the new rules'.

'Why are you allowed out in the evenings unchaperoned if you are to stay pure? Surely they should be scared that you may be attacked or raped or worse?'

'I may not be very worldly wise and I have not been out of my home surroundings until these last few weeks but I have been taught properly. I shall not get to see much of the world after the summer solstice so it is best I fit all I can into this short space of time. There is so much to see and do and I would like to be greedy and do it all'.

I know there is much she is not telling me about the future that is planned for her and for me. Some may call it our destinies. I get the feeling in the short while that we have spoken that I should like to know her better. I should also probably not even be speaking with her. It is a good thing it is me though and not someone unaware of her situation. Why should the verse from Proverbs 1 verse 17 enter my head with such force *Stolen waters are sweet and bread eaten in secret is pleasant*. I fear that I am having lustful thoughts about her. To admit this even to myself I should be sentencing us both to an early grave. I am the lover in the card having to make a choice between Miss Rose and 'The Dragons'. I know that choice is already made for me, but it cannot stop me wanting to protect her from the inevitable conclusion. *For there was no corruption in his will. No bent or inclination to evil, for that is sin proper and truly so called*. I must not think about her other than to be there to help and to prevent too terrible a fate.

'Well Miss Rose what shall we do tomorrow night? There is indeed so much to see'.

'Tomorrow is Sunday and I have a half day to myself as well as the evening. I should like to visit the *Botanic Gardens* and the dome. I read that there are many exotic plants and some which are not normally found in this country'.

Escorting Miss Rose to her feet it dawns on me that her name has not been chosen by a botanist at all but that it symbolises the fact that she must stay pure. Lilies are white mostly and the blood red of the rose, therefore she is not just the chosen rose but the white rose. She is pure blood. I help her on with her cloak and I agree that I should like to escort her to the gardens but first of all I should make sure she returns home safely.

'Mr. Black please just walk with me to the end of the road I cannot be seen walking home with you. Tomorrow I shall meet you at the place you stumbled upon me this evening, at 3 o'clock. There should still be plenty of hours left of light and hopefully not as many people about as they shall be attending churches, if that is convenient?'

I agree and leave her at the corner of the street I wait until she has entered the house and head in the direction of mine.

The evening had indeed turned out entirely different from what I imagined. Then again I hadn't really imagined anything passed finding out why she was living next door.

A good evening.

The best I had in many years and only one drink. The company had however made the evening what it had been and I found I could not wait until tomorrow. I did know that I was unconsciously having thoughts I should not have and no matter how much I would want to act on them I could not. *The carnal mind is enmity against God for it is not subject to the law of God, neither indeed can it be* (Romans Ch.8 v 7). I must get some sleep and try to prevent the inner voices taking over for I am in danger of wanting her for myself.

That night I sleep fitfully. I dream that she is beside me her soft skin against mine. Her bottom pressed against me as I find myself rising to the touch and heat of her. Her hair smells of flowers and I breathe in her scent as my hand finds the tip of one of her breasts I gently squeeze on her nipple. It hardens to the touch but she still sleeps. Slowly I move my hand further down over the curve of her belly to the hair just underneath. I move my hand further down and subconsciously she moves her legs to give me more access. I move my thumb over her mound and rub gently on the sensitive part just at the top. Two other fingers I rub in her wetness slowly she opens to me and I insert my fingers. She appears to feel me as she places a hand on mine as if to show me what way I should touch her. Slowly she rocks against my fingers and I feel her muscles spasm.

She then speaks 'I want you to hurt me like you do the others'.

In my dream state I tell her I cannot do that for it is not in my nature to create pain for others. She rolls me on my back and positioning herself on top of me she inserts my cock inside her, her eyes closed and her red hair wild as she rides me.

'Hurt me, please', she pleads. 'I need you to make me feel everything'.

I cannot.

'I need you to....... Without the pain I feel nothing, I want you to make me come alive. Mark me, bite me let me know that when I see my bruises that I once had some sort of feeling'.

She slides off my shaft and turns around her backside facing me and just says 'beat me'.

I can feel myself sweating as this is something I hate watching when at meetings. The men beating the women unconscious and knowing that they feel every stroke. I could never do that ......or could I?

This is different .....she wants me to hurt her.

I use the palm of my hand as I may do to a naughty child and I slap it against her ass cheeks.

The connection makes an imprint on her buttocks.

'Again' she says, 'make me feel it'.

Again I hit her this time a little harder, her ass bright red I hit her a few more times. Already due to the pale skin her buttocks are bruising. They are changing into colours which others may find attractive like an artists canvas. Those others aren't me and I worry I have gone too far.

'I cannot inflict more pain on you it isn't right' I inform her.

'Please do it, I like it. It gives me pleasure'. She takes my hand and places it between her legs. She is soaking and I know she is not lying. 'Take me hard and spank my ass at the same time'.

Just like I seen the other men do on the night of my first meeting. I instruct her to hold her buttocks apart as I slam my cock into her first slowly and then harder slapping her ass with both my hands and my balls. She screams 'harder, don't stop hurting me'. I feel myself getting close to release and I bend over her back, biting her hard immediately the blood rising to the surface of the skin. I pour myself into her and immediately I panic. Visions of men with swords appear at my window demanding to be let in. I do not move as I am rooted to the spot with fear both for myself and the fact I cannot protect 'The white rose'. The glass shatters and they take aim at my neck.

I wake up shaken as if I had just landed on the floor my feather mattress is drenched with sweat and I pray that my bedroom wall is thicker than the back of my fireplace. I am sure I was screaming in my sleep. I just hope I did not call her name.

The next day is dull. I cannot settle to anything. Three o clock felt like it would never arrive. I put one of my best suits and overcoat as it is chilly and on Sundays most people made an effort to dress properly. I met her at the corner of *Castle Street* as agreed. She was very elegantly dressed in a blue satin dress with matching shoes. They were the same colour as her eyes. This clandestine meeting was supposed to go unnoticed; I feared that every person we would meet would notice her. She could stand out in a crowd without even trying. I had planned to walk the mile to *Botanic Gardens* but I decided that it would be better to hail a carriage at the end of *Hercules Place*.

We headed straight up the road passed the more Bohemian houses of Botanic and Queens University, the carriage dropping us at the *Lisburn Road* side of the gardens. I asked her was there any specific reason that she wished to visit these gardens when there were others scattered around the outskirts of Belfast. Apparently she had always loved the garden at the house where she had resided for most of her younger years. There were however some species of plant which she had not seen in person before and should like to view them in the gardens and dome. Some of the local papers had apparently listed a selection of the plants that could be viewed in *Botanic Gardens* and it included some from rare ones from Portugal.

We walked at a leisurely pace until we came across *The Palm House* it was designed by Charles Lanyon and opened in 1839, the dome was an additional extension added in 1852. There had been a national boom in garden horticulture in Britain and it was very fashionable to keep public display gardens. This was Belfast's attempt at keeping up with the fashion.

We tried the doors and found them locked. A man walking in the other direction shouts across at us, 'the buildings are only open on certain holidays now you'll be out of luck on a Sunday anyways'. I nod my head with thanks at the information.

Not having ever had the pleasure of walking around the garden or buildings before I found I was a little disappointed at not getting to view the reason Miss. Rose was so eager to visit. We pressed our faces up to the glass walls of the house and could see a few of the plants. There were colourful specimens of all manner of colours. Miss Rose informed me there were 'bird's of paradise, frangiapani and some sort of cinnamon plant as well as flowering vines. I may have been brought up on a farm but I did not know a lot about actual plants and flowers. It was normally a woman's place to know all the different flowers, their colours and the meaning of each flower and colour. They would then take cuttings as my mother had often done and press them so they were dry and flat. They could then use them in their diaries or as book mark. My mother could not read so they often ended up as part of a picture.

Drawing ourselves away from the window, she says, 'I shall have to come back another day as I really would like to view the plants which are locked out of sight. One of them a rare orchid only blooms once every 23 years. The dome is quite fascinating though how do they get the glass to make such a circular shape. It is a great idea to accommodate some of the taller plants. Let us view the rest of the outdoor plants while we are here'.

The gardens are rather large in size and stretch back as far as the *Ormeau* area of town. We walk on the newly fashioned paths around the other areas of the gardens. Even I know the names of some of the more common species found in Ireland. Foxgloves grew quite wild where I come from and often self seeded growing up all over the countryside. Purple seemed to be the most common colour of this plant. She informs me that the finger like flowers *digitalis purpurea* are poisonous and can often kill an adult in hours if it is ingested. It may be pretty but can also be lethal.

It is turning into quite a warm afternoon and I remove my coat. She seems unflustered by the heat even in the buttoned up bodice of her jacket. It buttons to the neck and must be stiflingly warm. I had always thought that red haired people did not like the heat. We rounded a corner at the top end of the path to begin our return journey. We can hear children and see them picking berries from a hedge. Eagerly pulling handfuls the children appear to be very hungry. They look vaguely like blackcurrants although the leaves and shape of the hedge are not the same.

Miss. Rose shouts at the children.

'Don't eat the berries'. But they pay no heed. She runs over to them knocking them out of the nearest child's hand. But she is too late. Two of the others have already eaten the berries.

'We must make them sick', she shouts at me. 'Put your fingers down his throat'.

The children not having a clue who we were and thinking us mad made to run off. I grabbed the nearest and held him. By the urgency in her voice I gathered what they had eaten was poisonous.

She asks him 'how many did you eat?'

The child replies, 'only a few', not having a clue how to count. The children appeared to be poor and they had thought it a good thing to come across berries in the garden. I tell him to stick his fingers down his throat and make himself sick. Retching up what looked to be about four berries still intact the boy asks what will happen to his sister.

Miss Rose replies, 'these bushes are called *prunis luscitanicus* or cherry laurel. They smell like almonds and can often be mistaken for bay leaves. It is an evergreen shrub, which means it grows all year. The fruit which you have mistaken as berries are more often green than purple. They contain cyanide, which is poison, if your sister as ingested more than four or five berries she is dead already. If not you must make her sick, she cannot keep the berries in her stomach. Do you understand?'

The boy nods and runs off as fast as his short legs can carry him.

I notice she is rather flustered now and her satin bodice has sweat staining her armpits. That will be rather hard to remove. She is downcast and just says, 'she is most certainly dead'.

'How did you know that the berries were poisonous?' I ask.

'I had read about the plant in one of my books. Children and the poor often mistake the plant as food and are dead in minutes. The plant itself originates from Portugal and must be able to flourish here without the heat provided by the glass dome'.

'I must remember to stay on the good side of your humour Miss Rose. You know far too much about poisonous plants'. She looks away and begins to walk. Perhaps I had gone too far in my jest.

We walk a distance in silence. Then I suggest as it is passed tea time that we should get something to eat in one of the public houses. There are no carriages to be seen at the front of *Queens University* when we reach the road. We therefore walk towards the centre of Belfast. She is no longer in a good humour and I did not wish to make matters worse. All sense gone I am certain she will be noticed. Perhaps I am being overly cautious after all how many members of 'the dragons' would know this lady in person.

After walking almost a mile I am sure her feet are sore in the satin heeled shoes. I see *The Crown* bar ahead and offer that we should perhaps get food there. There are very seldom ladies of good quality in the public houses around Belfast I am glad that there are individual booths with doors to provide privacy. Otherwise Miss Rose would be receiving some unwanted attention by the locals who had been drinking all day.

The façade of the bar is very finely decorated with mosaic patterns and tiles. I escort her into the bar and ask the publican if we could use one of the booths. I give him a coin and he clears the one closest to the door. At least we will be closed away from prying eyes for a little while.

These booths are very upmarket containing individual bell pulls for service. Since it is a Sunday afternoon they have a roast lamb dinner on offer. We both order this and a small ale each, so much for me staying off alcohol. Unfortunately I did not dare drink the water they may offer and the ale seemed the safer option. She seems to have calmed down a great deal after the walk. Removing her outer jacket and gloves she sets them to the side. I let her know we could always go to *Botanic Gardens* another day during the week perhaps when the buildings are open.

'Indeed Mr. Black that would be nice, I am sorry the incident with the children had me rather frightened. I am not used to dealing with them. Perhaps we should have checked on the matter further? Also please call me Lily it is dreadfully tedious to abide by such etiquette we both know we are slaves to the rules at all other times. It should be nice for a time to relax a little'.

'Lily it shall be. If I am honest after the incident yesterday and what seems like a lifetime of keeping secrets I am afraid I have become immune to providing help for others. It is not that I do not wish to, but I have found that the many do not appreciate prying eyes. I am rather fond of my eyes. Apparently they are my best feature', I say teasing and batting my eyelids.

'Your eyes are indeed very blue and despite your jest they are indeed very striking. The eyes of an old soul some may say, as if they have seen a hundred lifetimes and felt the pain of each. You should not take everything so seriously'.

Smiling at her for being too intuitive and because I had thought the same of her I reflect that, 'I have indeed felt and seen several lives worth of pain but not all of my own. Since my wife and son died I have become somewhat of a recluse despite only being thirty years old. I do admit I am somewhat of a bore, favouring my own company and that of a bottle of *bushmills* whisky to that of women or other men. It has been a long time since I have enjoyed or indeed sought the conversation and companionship of others. There is something about you however that has me captivated and not in the same frame of mind as normal. My thoughts these last couple of days have been that of another for they defy logic. I am captivated by your face and your hair and your quick mind. Due to our fated destinies and the knowledge that you indeed know more about the way of life and men than you should. I must say I am for the first time in years wanting to feel the touch of a woman. Not that I have not had several women as you are very aware, but this time I want you to want me. I want you to invite me to touch you and know that you only want me and not half a dozen other men with whips and chains. Their mark made upon you, your mind and body scarred for eternity. I want to make my mark on you but only on your heart. Perhaps I am being too forward but perhaps our acquaintance shall be too short and I should regret not saying as I feel. My thoughts and feelings are another facet of myself I have not shared in years for fear of retribution'.

I stop talking and realise that she is red with embarrassment and unsure what to say in return.

'I apologise I have said too much Lily'.

The sudden silence allows me to hear the dull roar of revellers in the rest of the bar and brings me back to reality. The confines of the booth had me forget we were in company.

The publican arrives with the meals and ale and provides a much needed respite from conversation. We both tuck in and I realise I have not eaten much since the night before last and I am quite hungry. Lily has made me lose my appetite for anything but her.

Having finished her meal she stares at her plate as if mulling over what way she should say something. The way you get when you know there is no easy way to say something but it needs said anyway.

'Mr. Black I am unsure how to deal with what you have said. I have not had to deal with feelings of others in my forced confinement. I am very aware of what happens between men and woman as I have been made to witness the social gatherings of the order on several occasions as a threat to what will happen if I do not obey orders. However, nothing may come of your desires for you know I cannot be touched. This does not mean that I am indifferent to your protestations but I cannot encourage them. We will both face a certain and unpleasant death if anything were to happen. It is best that you try to dampen your fires or we shall both burn'.

'I am aware that what I said would have repercussions I am also unsure where what I have laid bare of my soul has come from. It is not like me to divulge anything never mind my deepest thoughts and these ones have come as a shock to me also. Let us enjoy each others company in what time we have but know that if our fates had been different and our paths crossed in a different lifetime I would be wanting more than friendship. It is as I said a long time since I have not had company of any description other than what I have been forced to endure. I want nothing more from you than what you can give'.

She looks at the now empty plate, then raising her eyes shyly but not her chin she says, 'my life is as this empty plate and I have nothing to give, should it be full I would gladly let you feast. You cannot let your palate become accustomed to the taste of this food for eaten meat should soon be forgotten, lest we should be left with a bitter taste in our mouths. Like the berries some things are better looked at and lusted after rather than satisfying our hunger. Do you not agree?'

'Lily, you say 'our hunger'? Does that mean you feel the same way? We have known each other only hours and yet I feel that I have known you a lifetime. I do not agree but I do not desire to suffer the consequences of disobeying the higher council. I should still like to meet with you while it is permitted. I think I should go out of my mind if I could not see you. We have two choices, we can live by the rules, or we can die by them. I should not bear to be the cause of your death'. I lift her chin with my hand so that I can look into her eyes. They seem to betray everything she thinks. The wary eyes as her tarot was read, the excitement and intrigue of the theatre and the frightened and sad eyes as she watched the children with the berries. Her eyes now show something else. Do I dare to think they show desire?

Looking into her eyes I reach forward and kiss her. Her lips were soft and I could feel her pull her chin slightly away from my hand before changing her mind. She kissed me back unsure at first and then she gave in to what she wanted. Pulling away I see the flush on her cheeks and the brightness in her eyes. Then in an instant the shutters cross her face and her mood changes.

'We should be getting back to our homes Mr. Black it is late and the master will be wondering where I am. It has been a lovely day for the most part, let us depart'.

I leave Lily in the booth while I go to the bar to pay our bill. There is such unique architecture in this building, the front of the bar resembles an altar and is finished with red mosaics. It is very opulent for a public house. I take in the interiors as I habitually have done since the first night in 'the big house'; the smallest details still fascinate me.

Smiling I pay the bill and head back to open the booth. I open the door and find that Lily is being pinned to the bench by a rather large man his hand across her mouth preventing her screaming. I have not fought in a while and would be no match for this fellow. I pick up the empty ale bottle and smash it over his head. Drunk as he may be the force does nothing. It does cause him to look behind him and gave Lily the opportunity to bite his hand. He reaches and slaps her across the face.

'Snobby bitch. Coming in here dressed like that you are obviously wanting paid for it'. He says before turning to me.

I can see from his eyes he isn't as drunk as I anticipated. Sober enough to spot an opportunity and enter the booth as I left. His hands come up to my throat and before I know what is happening I can feel the hands squeezing at my windpipe. I struggle to loosen his grasp with my own fingers but he is too big. My eyes start to swim and I am struggling to breathe. The next thing I know he loosens his grip and I can breathe in slow painful gasps. The man is lying on the floor screaming at the top of his voice like a castrati in severe pain. Blood is running in a puddle where he lies and I can see the broken bottom of the glass sticking out the top of his crotch. Lily was standing very still and very white her blue satin dress covered in blood. She had obviously grabbed the nearest weapon and stabbed him with it in the only place she could reach.

Standing still it is a while before I can quite fathom what has happened. The door of the booth ajar I realise others can see what has happened. They would have heard him screaming anyway. Lily now in shock and visibly trembling is sitting back on the bench putting on her outer coat. The publican comes to investigate the commotion and spots the man on the floor still groaning with the pain but not as audibly due to his loss of blood.

'Sir, I would ask that you and the lady do not leave yet until the constable has been called to attend'.

I know we cannot wait for the law to arrive as that would mean taking the details of both myself and Lily. There would be additional consequences for us both if we had to spend the night in the local gaol.

'It is quite clear what has happened here', I respond, 'this man has tried to assault the lady and she has defended herself. Perhaps if he regains consciousness then he will regret his actions more than he does already'. It was a matter of self defence.' Many of the other men here will not remember in the morning who was here and when. Save us all a lot of trouble and let us leave. The lady and I should not be dining together and she has suffered enough tonight without adding to her embarrassment. You'll have to get the man to the hospital to stop the bleeding but other than that it's just a bar fight nobody else witnessed'.

Lily is still visibly shaking grasping her clothes around her. The publican looks at her and back at me, visibly weighing up the consequences of each option.

'You better leave quickly and I suggest you get the lady home, she stands out too much in this area after dark. There are too many thugs about'.

I nod my thanks and put my arms around Lily's shoulders and usher her out the door into the now dark street.

We walk in silence until we get to the corner of *Donegal Street* taking a different route from when we had left this afternoon. At the corner I beg her to be careful and enter the house by the back door as it was still early enough for my neighbour to still be awake. Her dress would have to be removed or would surely see the blood stains and there would be questions as to where she got them. Before she leaves I ask her when she would like to go out again. She tells me that she is still in shock and cannot think straight, if she is going out during the week it will be late on but if she gets caught tonight she will not be allowed to leave.

I leave her at the corner and watch as she walks down the street and disappears from sight. Then I head towards my own home the words of William Blake's poem 'The Everlasting Gospel' entering my head *thy heavens doors are my hells gates.* He did mean that to one person heaven is hell not everyone worships the same way and to an atheist the idea of heaven is hell. My heaven has just left me to go home to her master and her fate; this is going to be my hell.

The Devil

It is often the things which we should forget that stick to the mind like glue. The obsession with a lover or an addiction we cannot fight, the touch of a woman's hand and the feel of whisky hitting the back of your throat.

The Devil is a card of metaphorical bondage. It depicts a man and a woman voluntarily shackled to the devil through their own ignorance. They have lost their independence through their own actions and there is a fear of the unknown due to limitations. This fear and submission give a feeling of hopelessness. The Baphomet looms over the couple, he represents the evils of sexuality and the suppression of sexual urges. He mocks the lovers who are attached by chains of love and ignorance, they are not victims but they are also not helpless. The man and woman have the means to release themselves from the captivity. There is always a variety of choices open to the couple. They must face the good with the bad as they cannot be separated. The dark must be taken with the light as it is impossible to separate a shadow from its source.

This card can be a sign to end a relationship or that lust has turned against them and that they should atone for sins which have been committed. These sins may not necessarily be physical but could be the result of an obsession or co-dependency. A sign you are hooked on something, that you have perhaps over indulged the senses on drugs for instance and you do not realise it, therefore you are prevented from being your true self. The couple are ignorant of the truth. This causes a loss of faith and a sense of self doubt, which is also reinforced by the Eight of swords by the creation of confusion and restriction.

There is always a sense of uncertainty with The Devil. People want what they cannot have and they feel ashamed of succeeding in their goals. Acts chapter nine tells us *His face towards hell, his back towards heaven, and therefore calls himself to turn. He loves what he should hate, and hates what he should love. Joys in what he ought to mourn and mourns for what he should rejoice in glorieth in shame and is ashamed of his glory.*

The night passes fitfully for I find that sleep is again neglecting me. There are so many things in my head. Mainly I wonder if Lily had been discovered entering the house in the state she was in, and if she had been caught, what would be her punishment? I do not know how I am going to be able to wait to see what the consequences of our interactions have been.

A day in the bank would hopefully keep me distracted. I pride myself on being patient but today I find it hard dealing with the awkward customers. I have no desire to enter into polite conversation and with each cheque I lodge the day seems to last longer.

Indeed the next few days pass in much the same fashion. I normally would revel in my own solitude spending endless days in a daydream of what my life could be like and what I could achieve if I were to discipline myself. My solitude these last few days has almost sent me mad. There has been no sign of Lily exiting the house and I find I miss her companionship. I am also growing increasingly concerned for her wellbeing. I do not even have a reason to call next door so that I may quench my curiosity. All I can do is bide my time and hope there is news soon.

On the Friday afternoon a letter is delivered with the dragon seal. It is unusual that the order have put their thoughts on paper. I open the scrolled paper cautiously, half afraid it will explode.

4th June 1858

You are hereby commanded to attend an exclusive and urgent meeting this evening. A carriage shall collect you at 7pm.

S

I have been waiting to be called for a meeting since Lily's revelations regarding my addition to the higher echelons of the order. I am however very dubious as to the reason for this meeting. I have a feeling this is not a good omen.

I am ready and waiting when the horseman arrives and it feels like I am waiting to be escorted by one of the horsemen of the apocalypse. I do not know whether it is War, pestilence or death for any of the three could be currently coming to taunt me with a fate worse than that of losing my life. Knots in my stomach I dread the thought of approaching the other members. Yet maybe I am being pre-emptive and there is nothing to worry about. Yet, I do not believe that for a minute. What if they know I was with Lily when she was attacked? What if I have been reported by my neighbour for entering his home without permission? What if I'm about to lose my head both literally and figuratively? What if......

I am in the carriage for over an hour. My linen shirt is stuck to my back like glue and I am glad I have two outer coats to hide my discomfort. The outer layers do not protect me from the chill of the evening and I shiver both from the cold and fear. Eventually the carriage comes to a halt at a large house which is surrounded by a forest on either side and a large sweeping driveway the sort favoured by rich men who had returned from a Grand Tour of Europe. Extensive landscaped gardens on either side of a long driveway provide a contrast to the darkness of the large Oak trees. Owners of such estates think that the duplication of European habits makes them appear more auspicious to their gentrified neighbours. It is a status symbol favoured to intimidate others. This evening it has the desired affect on me. My sphincter muscles pulsate in a tu'penny ha'penny rhythm and are adding to my discomfort. I am glad I have not eaten, for I am unsure which end I may find a surge of detritus from first. The surroundings fill me with a sense of foreboding. I exit the carriage and mount the steps; surrounded by the shadows cast by the outdoor lanterns I ascend to my fate.

I enter the building and everything is a blur. I let the man servant take my overcoat and greet him in a perfunctionary manner, going through the motions. I could describe it as going on a journey and returning home or reaching a destination without a notion of what happened in between. I cannot take in the details as I usually do, the architecture, the attention to detail of the interiors, the artwork or the furnishings for I am scared. I am ushered into a large dining room the table set for a meal, with thirteen settings. Most of these places are filled already except for the three closest to the door. The butler pulls out the one on the right hand side for me and I sit. Thankfully I do not have time to be introduced to the other guests as my neighbour and an older gentleman enter the room, the latter sitting at the head of the table and the neighbour opposite me.

The older gentleman stands and taps his glass as if to silence the already quiet guests. 'Gentlemen I am glad you have all been spared to congregate this evening. We are here for a celebration so please enjoy the food, the wine and the after dinner delights'.

I am too cynical to believe that I could now relax.

Seven women enter the room carrying the food and wine. They are dressed as what I could describe as either vestal virgins or Bacchanalian nymphs. The white flowing material drapes over their left shoulders exposing their right breasts and is almost opaque leaving very little to the imagination. I presume that none of them are virgins so maybe the term of nymphs is more appropriate. They serve the food in silence while two remain to refill the wine glasses as required. I settle slightly while I eat making idle conversation with the other gentlemen. Each man appears to have a different accent. One from the north of the country, another has a southerly one, each with their own colloquial twang. Obviously tonight's congregation are all from different parts of the country selected to be situated at a distance from each others normal habitat. This is ideal in preventing any of us bumping into each other on a regular basis.

I am always unsure of what is a suitable topic for conversing at any of these occasions and tonight I am wary of saying anything. I fear I may inadvertently sign my own death warrant. I therefore answer only when questioned and give the odd nod of agreement as I see appropriate.

My neighbour turns to me in the middle of the meal and says, 'I believe that you had the unforeseen pleasure of meeting our bride?'

'I am not sure of who you are referring, nor am I sure what you mean by our bride. You are aware I lost my wife some years ago', I reply hoping that my feigned ignorance is believable.

'The maid that showed you out of my home last week, she is to be our gift to the Almighty she is to become his bride'.

I am at present unsure what on earth he is talking about and in terms of the 'Almighty' it resembles what Lily had said on the night of our first acquaintance about being engaged to 'the Lord'. I may be slow on the uptake but I am almost certain they are not talking about God almighty. 'I do vaguely remember being shown out of your home by a youngish redhead. However as for the Almighty and brides that is going to have to be explained to me because I have no knowledge of what you are speaking'.

The neighbour continues, his ruddy complexion glowing in the light the grease shining on his forehead.

'Our female subject shall be sacrificed on the holy day of the summer solstice to show that we are still loyal subjects to our master Abaddon. We shall feast and drink of her blood so that his strength runs through our veins. This is a sacred event for it is only celebrated by the chosen few once every twenty eight years. Only our leader,' he indicates the older gentleman, 'has had the pleasure of attending the last event'.

The older gentleman appears to be uncomfortable with this conversation and does not acknowledge or deny the statement. I am also distressed by this declaration I am nauseous as my heart hits the floor at about the same time my stomach heads to my throat. I control myself enough to not actually vomit. I must not show any sign of weakness in front of these men. My thoughts are racing they intend to sacrifice Lily and then drink her blood in some sort of satanic ritual. Debauchery, orgies and slaves I can cope with, or rather have learnt to endure, but the thought of losing the one person who I have ever connected with in my life is too much and for that I may personally be capable of murder.

There is no way I will let her be sacrificed.

I do not know where she is so how can I help her.

My already damp shirt is now sticking to my back and I feel the beads of sweat on my brow. How is it possible that through one minor mistake as a boy I am now party to the most sinful of atrocities and I am sure I have committed all of the seven deadly sins and broken most of the 'Ten Commandments' since my first step into hell. It is possible that before I am content I may have broken all of the commandments for right now I wish to kill every one of these pompous, slimy, avaricious men and if one of them lays one finger on her I shall 'swing for him'.

I am dragged from my ruminations by the awareness that the elderly gentleman to my left has risen from his seat. He begins to talk but not as loudly as previously. 'Gentlemen I am sure you are wondering the reason for our celebrations. Many of you are aware that we shall soon celebrate the summer solstice and for all of you this will be the first sacrificial ceremony that you will attend and my last. We have added a new member to the ranks this evening and would like to welcome him. This does mean that as there are now thirteen members someone will be leaving our ranks'.

I can feel the temperature drop in the room.

I fear that the only way I am now to become a member is through the removal of another and that can only mean one thing. Someone is about to be removed permanently from the present company. Thirteen is indeed going to be someone's unlucky number.

The elder moves from the head of the table and starts to walk slowly along the back of the chairs at the opposite side of the table. He continues to talk.

'Therefore I have had to make a decision and due to recent events my decision has been made easier than I anticipated. It is however ironic that the very man who suggested our new initiate is the man who he shall be replacing'.

I automatically look across the table at my neighbour and see the once ruddy complexion has turned an off shade of grey.

'You are all very much aware that everything that happens between these four walls is sacrosanct. Nothing that happens or is said can be repeated to anyone else not even other members. The Rose has already been plucked; she was left in the capable hands of one member in the month preceding the ceremony. Unfortunately our respected gentleman does not know how to look after her properly. He also has no respect for keeping elements of the events he would participate in to himself. It is therefore his duty to renounce his post as protector and his place on this council'.

The elderly member now stands behind my neighbour. He reaches into the left breast pocket of his suit and pulls out what appears to be a letter opener. In a matter of seconds he puts one hand under my neighbours chin and pulls his head back and with the other he cleanly pulls the blade once across his throat. The startled expression remaining on the dead mans face as the blood from his carotid artery oozes from the wound and then sprays myself and the closest men to him. Without even hesitating the elder member wipes his blade on the napkin and replaces it in his pocket, he then continues to talk.

'Virgil as you have taken this mans place on the council you will now take up his responsibilities'.

He claps his hands twice and one of the women leave the room. In a matter of seconds she returns with Lily in pursuit. Lily tentatively wobbles on heeled shoes and her eyes are glazed. She is barely dressed in a corset, not of my design, and stockings. She looks at me and I am sure, had she not been certainly under the influence of drugs that she would have by just one look made the rest of the audience aware of our familiarity. She had obviously been made to use belladonna on her eyes as they are dilated and very bright. Belladonna is a drug distilled from the plant *atropa belladonna* a member of the tomato family but dangerous and containing scopolamine and hyoscyamine which cause delirium and hallucinations. I do not believe that Lily would voluntarily have used such vanities on herself, there appears to have been a heavy dosage used that far exceeds that of cosmetic use. Her pale almost opaque skin is covered in bruises and I find it hard to resist the urge to leave my seat and reach out for her.

Instead I remain glued to my chair and stare.

My eyes only leave her as I am told by the gentleman that it is now my responsibility to look after Lily until the night of Summer Solstice. I see this as more a pleasure than a chore. However, given that there is some time left until the event I am not sure I can promise to keep my hands off her. Certain I want no one else hands on her either I rise from my chair.

'Perhaps then gentlemen I should take my leave and take my charge home?' I ask this as a question so that I do not seem to be taking control from the elder. I fully intend to leave with Lily this minute no matter what the consequences. Yet despite my apparent bravery I am clenching my nails in the palm of my hands and hoping for a speedy escape.

'Mr. McAuley's house has been prepared for your arrival and your work has been informed that you shall be taking a short leave of absence. Take her there and we shall contact you if necessary'. Inwardly sighing with relief I escort Lily to the door of the room. I lead her out through the threshold and close the door behind us. Then with only the eyes of the servants upon me I take a better look at her. She is so very pale and very, very cold. This is not surprising given her state of dress and the fact that the weather has been cold for this time of year. She leans towards me unsteadily looking at my face and cupping it in her hands.

'You have very deep eyes you know. Deep and kind...... I want you to drown me......drown in your eyes.....I am already dead....I cannot breathe....suffocated.....you make me stop breathing'. She confuses her words sounding almost like her heroine *Ophelia,* I read between the lines and the meaning. I demand her clothes and soon have her wrapped up warm and heading into the awaiting coach. The two horses dancing between their reigns as they patiently await their commands. Perhaps they are also uneasy and unsure of what is coming next.

The journey takes longer than I expected or perhaps it is just the time of night and the impatience to be way from the prying eyes of others. Lily lies against my shoulder her head jolted by every bump in the road. She sleeps fitfully every now and then mumbling something in her drug induced sleep. Eventually we reach our destination; it seems strange to be approaching this house after so many years and in this fashion. I had arrived on foot the few times I had been here, and have not been in the neighbourhood at all since Emily's death.......or that of my parents.

The butler helps me to take Lily up the stairs to her chambers. Oil lamps dimly light our path and on entering the room I realise this is the room in which I spent my wedding night. The same Egyptian style bed in the centre of the room where I awoke to find the scarification of my arm and the words etched on my skin for eternity, mit blud und gehorsam'. How much blood had been spilled since that day? How many lives ruined and changed beyond recognition? How many had failed to obey? Yet here I am again blindly following orders. I have a feeling that I only thought my life had changed up until now. There is the uneasy and subconscious feeling that this is the beginning of the rest of my life. Everything will change from tonight.

The butler leaves and I am left alone with Lily. She lies unconscious across the bed. The scene vaguely resembling that of Fuselli's painting 'The Nightmare'. I remove her outer garments with difficulty as she is dead weight in my arms. Leaving just her corset and under garments I lie her on the bed, and watch the rise and fall of her breasts as she sleeps and the flickering of her long lashes on her cheeks. She does not resemble the strong confident young woman she portrays while she is in full control of her facilities. She looks fragile and in need of love and affection. Tired I remove my shoes and lie down beside her.

I am worried about Lily's reaction in the morning, to tonight's events. William Blake's words rattle around my head. *O the cunning wiles that creep, in thy little heart asleep. When thy little heart doth wake. Then the dreadful night shall break.* Despite trying to fight sleep I drift off into the darkness.

The clock chimes midnight and out of the nowhere five figures appear floating in the mist. Four men naked and a woman suspended by cloth between them. Their hands grab at her from every direction pulling her as if she should be quartered. The faces of the men display their pleasure as they bring pain to their tethered prey. Her head tilted back writhing trying to escape but her ankles and wrists are held firm. She appears to be almost suspended in time being pulled in four different directions. Their hands, fingers and tongues touch every part of her. Opening her at their touch, spreading her legs they each with cock in hand prepare to take her, she belongs to them and can do nothing to change that. The woman stops writhing and fighting for escape. Bound, trapped and resigned to the fact that she cannot stop them her body lies limp between her bonds. My blood runs cold with rage as each man in turn makes her his own, raping her, defiling her and filling her with their demonic seed. I cannot stop them as I remain pinned to the ground my arms trapped and I tremble. She is mine they cannot have her.

I awake feeling cold, still on top of the bed covers, Lily's eyes still shut beside me. I remove my arm from under her head. She opens her eyes slowly, the half light in the room making her squint. In a similar fashion to myself after a few too many spirits.

'Where am I and why are you here? Why are you bleeding' she croaks.

'I shall get you breakfast on a tray and then we shall discuss what has been happening since we last met'. I had forgotten the other man's blood on my face and feel a sudden urge to wash before bringing Lily her food.

Leaving the room I ask the servants if it would be possible to have breakfast taken up to the ladies chambers as she is still rather fragile. Not having packed any of my own belongings for the journey here; I ask if I have any clothes to change into and if I could have a bath made up so that I may wash off the outer stains of last nights events.

The bath water is tepid but I did not want to give them time to fill it completely from the scullery. I wash and dress myself as quickly as permitted without rushing as I am still fatigued. Then I head back up to see Lily.

Sitting upright against the bolster the tray sitting over her lap she smiles slightly as I enter the room. My own breakfast sits by the side of the fireplace and I feel I must eat before we can talk properly. I did not consume much of last night's meal and I am now hungry. Covering the bread with butter and honey, I then pour myself a cup of tea. All in silence, but I can feel her eyes watching me and internalising everything. I finish eating my own food then stand up and remove the tray from across the bed. I then sit beside Lily on the edge of the bed…..not touching her.

'How are you feeling?' I ask.

'My head hurts a little and my eyes are blurry, they made me use those drops in my eyes. I would have come willingly but that man I lived with beat me when I arrived home last week. I could not find a way to let you know as I was locked in the upper bedroom. He accused me of being with men and that if he had known I would be a harlot he would have taken me himself, except for the fact that he prefers his neck in one piece to bringing down a whore. He would not be saying anything of my escapades to anyone else as it would reflect badly on him but I had now lost my freedom to explore the rest of the city. I did not feel much loss at being confined except for my desperation to be in contact with you …….' her eyes wide she looks at me waiting for a response.

'I've missed you and I was worried about you and I know that I may appear to have lost my senses. We had such a connection when we met that I wish that we could have met in another life. I valued every second of our conversation and time together and I did not want to let you go back to that house. I am normally a grounded person in terms of my responsibilities and the reality of our situation.

I've tried so hard not to be distracted from everything that I am meant to be focussing on, but when I met you I just couldn't help myself. There is definitely going to be trouble and you could do without that in your life. I however, no longer care what is thrown in my direction as long as I get to be in your company'.

'How is it possible to meet a stranger and talk for hours that seem like minutes and have to walk away not wanting it to stop, but yet knowing that it must. In most cases talking to the tombstones of the dead is preferable to talking to those who feign interest as their eyes glaze over. I have not had much companionship these last few years but I do know I've never met anyone who I would follow straight into hell just for their conversation and company'.

'I really feel like I've known you all my life and talking to you and being in your company has been a rare pleasure. It's amazing how feelings can emerge and develop in such a short space of time and they don't take into consideration circumstances. No one has been able to converse with me about anything and everything before. No one until I met you and within a matter of moments I knew you were someone I was meant to meet and form a unique bond with, I am fascinated by you and I have not even scratched the surface yet. You have stirred within me emotions which I did not even imagine existed; I feel things I have never felt before. I want to look into your mesmerising eyes and feel the desire to kiss you and know that I can. In your company we can turn some hours into other people's lifetimes.

If I was to say to you that we are in possession of a box, but not just any box, Pandora's box[7]. That together we have the keys to open it and that the decision to

---

[7] Pandora : Zeus demanded that Pandora be created out of clay with beauty and cunning, her name means to bare all gifts, but she is not a gift but a punishment. She was supposed to be a form of punishment for her future husband Epimetheus brother of Prometheus. Zeus sent Pandora as a gift to Epimetheus who was immediately smitten and asked her to marry him. At the wedding Pandora is presented with a box (which was probably more the shape of a Greek urn) at her wedding. She was told never to open the box. Almost like Eve in some ways in Greek myth she is the first woman who is tempted by her curiosity, longing and desire just like Eve in the 'Garden of Eden'. Their free will gets the better of them and they suffer the consequences of their individual actions. Pandora releases the evil spirits from the box and the last thing to emerge from the box was hope. It is my personal opinion that

leave the box closed or to open it lies solely with us. I do not want to destroy the box but by opening it we will break the chains of entrapment and the power of our oppressors. We will also unleash any demons which care to follow us over the threshold, into the world of our dreams, into the land of our imaginations. I live for this darkness but I am scared of what the demons will do to you. What if I said I had already opened this box, in my dreams, not just once but repeatedly since we met. I know what the box has in store and once it is opened there will be not going back, only forward, for fate has given us this choice and I want to unleash the demons. They cannot be worse than the ones we already fight. It is also said that the box contains 'hope' but did Zeus place it there as a blessing or a curse. Do we hope for a happy ending or the ability to do as we desire? Dare we hope for life?'

'If I was to say that you are wrong it is not us both that possess the key, but I, through my voice. You cannot open the box alone and you are waiting for my response and my permission. If I do not speak then I can never express what is inside of me, forever, or until my death, suppressing my voice never letting myself think or feel what I want, and I want you. Is that what you want to hear? I have never wanted anything in my life, never desired anything that others had, until now. Now the only thing I ever wanted or needed is in front of me offering me a lifeline, giving me the opportunity to have the only thing I have ever desired. Through my voice we open the box and shake off our chains and I do not want to lose this opportunity to be with you and in your company. Indeed there is hope, but I do not for one minute presume that Zeus meant it as a blessing. All I ever hoped for was you and your company and I knew within minutes of meeting you that fate had brought us together. The lovers in my tarot reading destined to be joined by our own volition to the chains of the devil. Let us open the box and suffer the consequences for I should rather face the demons of the future than regret having never lived. You are not the only one who has dreamed.

Do you believe in the prospect of reincarnation, the possibility and knowledge that we have been here before in a past life. The unexplainable moments of déjà vu when you are certain you have lived this moment of your life before and that you hope was not meant to be good but evil that Zeus placed it in the box as an additional punishment for Pandora's disobedience.

can tell exactly what is going to happen and what each person will say or do next. I often have the same vivid dreams over and over throughout my life the same dreams occurring; the first which I have had since I was around five years old occurs at a grave. There is a large grey cross so high against a blazing red sky that it cast shadows over the line of people waiting beneath its heavy bows. Soldiers stand at the head of the grave. The men and women opposite wait to find out if they shall be the next occupant of the grave, each person in line falling deep into the bottomless depth, toppling over the cliff edge into a black nothingness. I come to my turn in the queue and I can fall into the grave or take a leap of faith and jump over it. Each time I jump the dream ends and I wake up sweating both from fear and the heat of the sun.

The second dream I have had for nearly as many years. It is the year 1589 I do not know how I know this but as I dream it is set in my head. In this dream I have a bird's eye view of my surrounding area. It is a large open square area or piazza surrounded by the finest objects of architectural grandeur. These Buildings we can now only dream of erecting, dwellings literally built with blood, sweat and tears and possibly a few bodies thrown into the foundations for good measure. To my right there is a large building approximately fifty yards squared. Its roof is supported by eight pillars each pillar has grooves in the masonry so that it is not completely rounded due to the scalloped edging. One central wooden door tall enough to accommodate giants provides both an entrance and an exit to the building and in this case, people are running from the mammoth structure screaming, others lie dead on the steps. In front of me there is a large monolith the eye of Horus winking back at me through the black tendrils of smoke engulfing a single figure. I can smell the smoke in my nostrils and taste the acid of the sulphur. I sweat with the heat of the flames. Then as if I have already wakened from the dream it hits me like the stabbing pain in my chest. The figure is me. Bound but not silenced. I am looking down on myself and my own death. The flames of the pyre tear at my flesh and my redhair now the colour of fire itself burns brightly as if kissed by the sun and Satan has come from hell himself to claim me.

In the midst of the pandemonium a single dark haired figure stands with his back to my current position, watching and waiting. The stake in my heart falls free with my flesh and I know that although we have never met that I know him. He isn't waiting for my death but my rebirth. There is a silence despite the noise and frenzy of all that surrounds us. It is as if I have finally returned to the beginning of time itself. Each time I am reborn I come a step closer. This has happened before and will happen again not in the same way but we will be reborn and the figure and I will eventually meet.

I have spent hours in the libraries of the large houses I have lived in, looking in the artwork for the location in my dreams. It is too vivid to be a dream, it is more of a memory and as I awaken each time I taste the sulphur and smell the burning. I spend hours reading the diaries and memoirs of those who have toured Europe, as the place was not in Ireland it had the style of an Italian temple or Greek Pantheon. I found a print in one of the books of an Italian piazza and as my eyes took in the baroque artwork on the page, my hands shook and my heart raced and I knew I had been there before. The Piazzo del Popolo swam before my eyes as if it had been yesterday. It was a much darker place than portrayed in the colourful imagery in the painting, decaying corpses, flames, plague, fire and the rotting flesh. The Baroque image in front of me is too bright, too cheerful. Yet in the very depths of my soul I knew I had been there, lived there and waited.

It is you I have been waiting for through many lives. I have been told I have an old soul. Perhaps I do. It is time to share all that is in my soul with someone and much of it belongs to you now, let us unlock the rest, together'.

Although I have looked for it in others I have never seen such honesty in someone's eyes and I know that she means everything that she says. I do not know how to control my emotions and everything that I now feel inside me. My heart races and my hands shake as I move myself up the bed so that I am now at her side. Taking Lily's hands in mine I lean over and kiss her not as tentatively as the first time as I feel a fire in me that is burning me up and I do not know how to control the flames. She kisses me back and I know that this fire is only starting to flame that before it is contained we will both be consumed by an inferno that we have no intention of fighting.

I try to control myself for Lily's sake and I withdraw from her lips kissing her on the forehead and again sitting at the end of the bed. After her ordeal she is not ready for anything else. If there is more than just kissing and we were to make love to each other, am I prepared to suffer the consequences?

Would I die for her?

I immediately conclude that I would follow her to hell and back and suffer whatever punishment I am given. I know that despite our short acquaintance that she is my life and without her I am dead already.

I leave Lily to rest a while and decide to walk around the house. Why shouldn't I have a nosey about, after all there is no one here to stop me. I am master of 'the big house' while I am here. Compared to my first visit I am free to wander around and look at whatever I want away from prying eyes. I start in the hallway taking in the frescos and furnishings. The crimson velvet drapes hanging from both the windows and the ceiling sconces. A stags head displayed on the wood panelled wall is reserved pride of place. It was possibly killed on the estate as there are quite a few deer around this area. Looking at it I feel there may be something in the air for when I think of Lily I feel like a stag in heat. Yet I must put all such thoughts from my mind after all there are many other types of intimacy. I try not to think of her in such a fashion yet I find it extremely difficult. She deserves more than to be treated like a deer in heat surrounded by a stag seeking a good night's sex.

Branching off the hall is the dining area where I had met Emily all those years ago. Awkward and embarrassed I blush at the memory. I also think with sadness at such a waste of a young life. Yet in her short time on earth she had probably experienced more than most individuals could hope, aspire or dread to want to feel, fulfilled. I know in her own way that she enjoyed her life. It may have seemed strange at the time but on reflection I realise she knew no other path. She had been brought up and indoctrinated in a certain way of thinking much like a zealot, politician or extremist. Emily therefore had no reason to question her actions regarding herself, myself or other women she recruited. We did not have long together but I grew to love her in some form. I miss our son more; an ache fills my heart as I think of how I left him on the doorstep, as if he was unloved or cared for when it could not have been further from the truth. He was my life at the time and the grief of his loss almost killed me. Only now am I starting to live again and avoid my one comfort of alcohol. If I am honest I think it is Lily who has kept me from the drink for all I can think of is her these past days.

Leaving the highly polished wooden surfaces of the rosewood dining table and the glinting silverware behind, I retrace my steps into the hall and head down the corridor to the drawing room. Memories of that November night again fill my head. The shame of my actions which had now lead me to this point in my life.

Do I regret having sex with Emily that night?

Yes.

Would I do it again if I was placed in the shoes of an eighteen year old me?

Yes probably.

Does this mean I should regret my actions?

I have regretted them nearly every minute of my life until now. I regret breaking the trust of my parents, of following the whim of a moment, of trusting a stranger… and yet if I had not done all these things I would not be who I am now in this moment. I would not have found something I had never experienced until this time. I would not have met Lily. How is it possible to have spent less than a day in someone's company and feel like you have know them a lifetime. When the reality is you have just met. How can the briefest of encounters change everything?

Even as I ask myself this I know the briefest of encounters can change everything, for bad too which is how I am now standing back in the very room where a spur of the moment decision changed my whole life. Perhaps it is fate and our lives are pre destined to turn out in a certain way. It may be the case we meet people for a reason, that we meet them when fate dictates and not before. Yet fate is fickle, uncaring and cruel. Very much like Zeus giving Pandora a box containing hope which is just there for his own perverse pleasure. Just a taste of something which could be good yet can be taken away from you in the blink of an eye. Hope is the desire for something good to happen with the greatest possibility it never will. Hope is an aching chest filled with dread and the butterflies of excited anticipation.

It is the possibility of love with the reality of loss. Hope is the in the hands of the Gods to distribute as their pleasure and to tempt us with all we desire. Hope is there to keep us going when all around us is fear and sadness, a reason to not take our lives in our own hands. It is like dangling a carrot in front of a donkey and no matter how many steps forward it goes it cannot reach its goal. Hope can vanish in a moment as if it never existed.

In my experience over the years it is not just hope that can vanish but with the right connections many other things can disappear too. The dragons can make anything disappear, consume all in their path and not leave so much as trace they were there. They had been successful in their task up until now……….

I sit on the end of the chaise. Perhaps it is the same one I sat on the night of my wedding. I do not know. I did not notice the colour or design. After I had blacked out from the pain of the branding iron I had not set foot back in this room. In daylight it appears plain. Not as grand as I remember. The walls are still adorned with the same paintings depicting dragons and temptation. The room itself does not have the same gothic allure as it does in the light of flickering oil lamps. The same warmth as provided by a roaring fire. I am surprised there is not one lit today despite the month. A house this size needs warmed even in June for the walls being as thick with stone they become damp easily. I stare at the walls for a time from my perch and then feel I should probably move.

At the end of the corridor is the large oak door which leads to the ballroom. The entrance into the den of iniquity where I had my first drink, my first game of cards and my first initiation into the depravity of man. Innocent then I did not realise that the depraved nature of men could be worse than alcohol and gambling. My parents had been right when they said the owner of 'the big house' did not follow the ways of the Lord. The room is not as big as I remembered. Perhaps that is because I have a better form and quality of living now and I have seen far grander homes. Perhaps it is because I am no longer scared and in awe of my surroundings. Leaving the room I head back down the corridor and into the hallway. Then I open the door on the right hand side, into a room I had never entered before.

I am at once surrounded by the sight of books. Big books, small books, old books......it is the smell that I immediately recognise.

The smell of knowledge......the smell of age.

The smell of old leather and that of dust layered paper and velum. At once I forget all else in my head and just gaze at the wall to wall books....it is like heaven. The large sash windows let enough light into the room that there could be no problem reading in the daylight. The other three walls are from floor to ceiling filled with books and manuscripts. I walk over to the nearest shelf and lift out the first red leather bound volume. I open it and place my nose to the pages and breathe in the familiar smell. I may not have been brought up in a home where we could afford to read but in latter years I have become accustomed to reading and to spending my time in the hours of the poets and scholars.

I have an absolute passion for gothic horror being totally drawn to he characters of Ann Radcliffe's *Mysteries of Udolpho* I had been hooked ever since. The fictional aristocrats and virginal heroines often gave me light relief from the more gruesome real life. Mary Shelley's *Frankenstein* I found extremely intriguing, that anyone would wish to bring a monster of different parts to life. Yet do we not face demons everyday and probably of a more cruel nature? The extreme diversity of Robert Louis Stevenson's *Strange case of Dr Jekyll and Mr Hyde* had me quandering the duality of personality and the meaning of life itself. Every day I watch people walk into the bank or eating at a restaurant and wonder to myself is this person just like Stevenson's character. Do they live their normal everyday lives and kiss their children good night, then go out to a Dragon's meeting and commit murder, fornications and adultery. I often feel the need to compare this concept with the stage masks of Melpomene and Thalia. When the ancient Greeks put on plays the players wore masks so that the audience could see their expressions more clearly. Hence we get the tragic and laughing faces, or perhaps the more apt expression two faced or showing another face. The fiction is a very welcome escape into a dreamworld and my imagination, there are times there is no other place I would rather be than living in the labyrinth of my own now twisted mind. Opening doors to a different reality and closing those of a more real hell.

Just as I notice a set of periodicals on the bottom shelf I sense a movement behind me.

'They are good you know', she says.

'What are?' I ask.

'The Penny Dreadfuls.......I had read a number of them when I was here before I absolutely love the feeling of suspense and the thrill of reading through one. The large houses, the dark gardens.......the heroines in distress.......'

She faded out as if she was referring to something else. Reaching over she removes the one that is now in my hand. Lifting it she holds it to her nose. Mimicking my movement moments before...... I smile to myself.

I thought I was the only person with strange habits.

'You really must excuse me', she states 'I absolutely love the smell of books. They just have one of those aromas that remind me of happy days, living in the depths of my mind. Living in the world of the characters and escaping from this reality. There is nothing like the images that each person can create from the same fiction. I really love the work of Shakespeare as you already know but it is a different kind of story that you find in the gothic horror. If *Ophelia* should appear in the work of Ann Radcliffe she should appear as a mad ghost haunting the rooms of an Italian Castle and fighting off the lovers of her brutal husband. I often wonder if the character of *Sweeney Todd* who appeared in *The String of Pearls* was a secret member of the order. He seemed to have their unbridled lust for slitting throats'.

I study her countenance looking for some sign of emotion or what she is feeling. I cannot read her.

'Perhaps we should have a discussion about what you experienced last night? I am sure it shocked you to see the barbaric nature of our masters'.

'Perhaps it would shock you, to know, that although I appear to be innocent of all things I have witnessed more in this short life than you could possibly imagine. Often I forget which of my nightmares are real or from my imagination. I have never turned to drugs for relief or of my own free will but I do understand how many women and men could wish to forget everything.

During my time at one of the other homes I was introduced to other girls. Other girls who had been chosen to fulfil the role of the chosen one. There was only one difference between us all......I had redhair. Luck perhaps intervened on my part for a change or perhaps fate. One of the men who had been researching the occult believed that I was the best choice due to my hair colour. It may not be the most fashionable colour for women in general at present but apparently it has more power and our blood is more pure. He quoted Cyrano de Bergerac to present his case, *A bravehead covered with redhair is nothing else but the sun in the midst of the rays, yet many speak ill of it.....their flesh much more delicate, their blood more pure, their spirits more clarified and consequently their intellects more accomplished.*

We were at first allowed to wander the house and grounds as we pleased just as we had always been permitted to do. Then one afternoon in late November a group of well dressed men herded us together and took us down a set of stone steps just off the scullery. The spiralling stairway took us straight to the bowels of the house. The corridor was lit by flickering candlelight and the rooms were nothing but prison cells. The place smelt of damp earth and iron. They had led us to a dungeon. Anyone visiting the premises would never have guessed that the place existed it was so deep beneath the upper floors. A shallow gulley ran the length of the corridor and straight into the cell at the end of the passageway. We had all followed without question like lambs being lead to the slaughter. Not entirely sure at the beginning what was going to happen we neither spoke nor struggled.

Things changed rather quickly.

Only one girl is required eventually for the rituals but a substitute was also needed in case of illness or death of the chosen one. The two of us were taken to the side and chained to the wall, the others taken from the room, then one at a time they were brought back and we were made to watch as in turn the young women were taken by the men. In the end I could not help but watch in stunned silence. Too scared to look away in case I could not see my own fate approaching. The girls in turn were stripped of their dresses, corsets and stockings, their wrists and ankles bound between two pillars. The men touched them at first groping their breasts, slapping their buttocks, their skin red raw. The chubby fingers of the men probing between their legs, hands touching them all over, squeezing and marking their flesh. The ankles still bound their hands were released so they could bend over, displaying their buttocks and private parts to the men behind. Hands now held behind their backs by one man another removed his hard cock from his breeches and in one swift move thrust himself inside. Some of the girls screamed in pain while others resigned to their fate remained mute and numb to the actions of their attackers. Another man at the front gripped the face of the girls between his fingers forcing their bulging eyes to look up at him as he forced his engorged penis into their mouths. Pushing himself so far inside them they turned purple from lack of breath. Then just as the girls thought they could breath no more the cock was removed just long enough for the girl to breathe before he started again. Tears streaming down their faces with the pain and shame of what they were enduring. Five, six, maybe seven men took turns on each girl riding them like they were animals, inseminating them as if they were no more than prize heifers on a farm. Then when they were done the limp bodies were again tied up by the wrists. The ones who had screamed were the first to go, in one swift move one of the men pulled their heads back and slit their throats. The blood spurted in all directions and ran into the gulley underneath them as if they were pigs at the butchers. The others, those who had remained silent were given a choice. They could remain alive and spend the rest of their days in solitary confinement in a room where they would entertain higher levels of the order as they were required while never repeating to anyone about the events of their life or they could end everything now......at the edge of the blade. *Sweeney Todd* would have been in his element.

Only one of the girls chose to live...... the rest were swiftly removed and the bodies taken away. All the time we watched knowing that we were being given an example of what would happen to us if we ever strayed from the crimson path. Crimson the colour of the dragon, the colour of their blood, the sky that night and thankfully the colour of my hair. Do not assume Virgil that just because I have remained a virgin that I am not aware of the very basest acts of lust and the perverse nature of human kind. I have witnessed more than even you, and I know more about what is to ensue than you. I have always been strangely resigned to the fact that I knew what was to come and I have accepted my fate.........at least until I met you. I really wish now that everything was more straight forward'.

Her blue eyes looked at me as if she could see into my very soul. I could tell she was taking in my reactions and I knew she had gauged a few of my thoughts although she did not acknowledge the fact. How could someone of the female sex endure as much and yet remain so calm and matter of fact. Although I had witnessed pain, rape and sex at many of the gatherings of the order a lot of the women were pleased to endure the pain. Even as a man I still could not get over the barbarity of the men and also hid my feelings as best I can. From Lily I expected delirium, perhaps madness but not a coldness that I felt hid a world of varying emotions. The only way I would ever truly know her feelings is if she wanted me to know and told me. That she has opened up just this little bit about herself was a major decision from her.

Sensing that we needed to move to a more cheerful topic I suggested that we should perhaps take a stroll around the grounds while the weather was good and before it was time for dinner.

The rest of the day was uneventful. We walked around the garden in a companionable silence adding the odd pleasantry regarding the plants and the architecture of the house I learnt nothing more regarding Lily's life and I did not tell her anything of mine but I wanted to share everything with her. I was troubled by her revelations but honoured that she should trust me enough to tell me her secrets.

I felt that she had confided with me all she was able to for one day. I know if it had been anyone else I would have been impatient for answers and probably have gone out of my way to learn more about her. Naturally inquisitive I would have questioned and annoyed her into clamming up altogether. Yet strangely I think patience and tolerance is what is required for her to let me in and to learn to trust me. Maybe it is because I found her to be so openly honest about everything in her life that I find I am able to give her space to be herself. I can see the honesty and emotion in her eyes and I know that whatever communication we have is something to be treasured. I need to be careful I do not want to lose the progress that has been made.

6th June 1858

My sleep was not as troubled last night I found that for the first time in a long while I am facing the morning more refreshed, less agitated and with a smile on my face in anticipation of what today has in store. I am surprised given that it was a strange bed and that I had a lot on my mind. I did however go to bed more at ease with my feelings and Lily was safe under the same roof as myself, therefore I suppose I had no need to be as anxious as usual.

I get washed and dressed and head down to the dining room for breakfast. The table is already set and I can smell bacon and bread frying in the kitchen. I take a seat at the long table and lift the copy of today's paper which has been provided. I scour the pages for anything of interest but take very little of it in, as my head is thinking of what I could do with my day. It may be an idea for Lily and I to take a walk into the town and visit Mr. Fox at the shop, if he is still alive. While we are there she could be fitted for a new dress or two. She may not need them long but I am determined to find someway out of this mess for us both......I am not optimistic.

Lily arrives down to breakfast dressed plainly in a brown shift dress and sensible shoes. It is like something my mother would have worn to church. She seems self conscious and comments 'nothing else in the closet fitted. The previous owner of the dresses must have been slightly smaller than myself and the corsets were just too restrictive'.

'It is a good thing then that I have decided that we should take a walk to the local milliners to get you fitted for some new dresses. Once we have eaten we will take a walk over the fields. Perhaps we should see if there is a pair of boots for you somewhere in the house. Those shoes will not be very comfortable for walking through grass. I don't want you getting blisters and sores on your feet'.

'Virgil today is Sunday the milliner will not be open'.

'I had forgotten.....the recent events have put my calendar out of pattern.....We shall do that first thing tomorrow. Today we will take a walk to my parent's house and along the river'.

Breakfast arrives in the form of bacon, bread and eggs. I am glad I did not have to cook, not having to do so means I can worry about other things. It has been a while since anyone has served me breakfast. I cannot be annoyed with servants at my own home and prefer to sort myself out much as I would have done as a boy. I just feel slothful when I rely on others to do things for me which I am very capable of sorting out myself. Normally I have very little else to do with my own time and I need to keep occupied. Today and for as long as I am at this establishment I shall, however, make an exception.

We eat in relative silence and wash the tea down with a pot of tea. Then I excuse myself from my chair and walk to the window. The weather is not great but the clouds do not hide rain from what I can tell. We should therefore be able to walk to the house and back without any problems. I ask the servant, who appears to be the same one that showed me into the house on the night previously, if there were any walking boots for Miss Rose. He lets me know he will have a look in the scullery and tack house to see if there are any of the appropriate size and not too well worn.

The man returns a little time later with a pair of small black ankle boots. They were probably more suited to a young boy but they will stop Lily hurting her feet or ankles when walking over the bumpy fields.

Some half hour later she returns to meet me in the hall wearing the boots. I fight back the urge to laugh as she is such as sight, in the boots, black stockings, brown dress and a really ugly frilly maroon velvet coat. If 'the order' had remembered to pack some clothes for me to travel in they should have had the foresight to cater for Lily's needs as well. Male chauvinists to the core, I am giving them credit for having the feeling and emotions to pack clothes for a woman. When I know she probably didn't even enter the tiny minds. Let us hope that we do not encounter too many of the locals on our outward journey. Most of them, I am sure probably do not even remember me but if they come across a lady dressed as she is the will not forget in a hurry. It's as if she dressed with the remnants of a pawn shop or fell off the back of the rag and bone cart. It might actually be an idea to visit the nearest pawn shop tomorrow to see if they have any matching clothes for Lily as it would be a few days before any new clothes would be stitched and ready to wear.

When leaving the grounds of the house we do not head down the driveway, it is a circuitous route and would be a lot longer than walking through the back fields. I therefore lead Lily around the side of the house to the back garden. We walk down the path which is surrounded by cherry blossom trees that are nearly at the end of their season. The petals pave our path as we head towards the back exit of the estate. On climbing the stile we head up hill through a field of cows and sheep, along the banks of the river towards the main road. There is not much to see on the outward journey but on the way back there will be a view for miles, over the hills and across the river valley. A perfect vantage point if we were to be attacked by an army.

The road is not as rough underfoot as the fields and a lot easier to walk on. I walk slowly to prevent Lily getting sore feet. The boots she is wearing are not new but they are not broken into her feet and are bound to be chaffing. She has not mentioned them but I think that she is just being polite. I inform her that when I was a boy I could probably have walked our journey up the brae and across the fields in less than a half hour. Now the last ten years of over indulgence and lack of a daily constitutional are taking their toll and I am finding I am sweating from the exertion. If I had run this journey as an eighteen year old I probably would not have broken a sweat. The walk is just about three miles and at our leisurely pace has us at the hill at my parents farm by half eleven.

The last time I made this journey I was on my way home to inform both my parents that I was getting married. I was filled with fear and sadness as I had walked down the hill to the yard. Today I am filled with a different sadness and a feeling of apprehension. I had not so much as thought of visiting the farm in ten years. I now owned it but I had no desire to be filled with the guilt of not being able to visit my parents before they died. Lily stands beside me as I look down on my smallholding.

'My parents lived in that house.......the last time I was here was the morning I got married to Emily, Samuel McAuley's daughter. I sat round the table with my parents and ate something similar to what we had this morning. Then we left for the wedding at the house and after the ceremony my parents came home. I had letters from them for a couple of years but I never visited. I was ashamed of my actions and how I had come to be married and my initiation as a member of 'The Dragons'. Neither of them knew anything of my treachery. The last time I heard of them was when the local vicar informed me they had both died of fever some weeks after my wife and child. I have had not had any desire to visit the house.....and I am still not sure I wish to venture further'.

'Perhaps it would be good for you to put some of your demons to rest. I would also like to see the house where you grew up. We must all approach our fears at some stage Virgil. Some of them are bigger than others and harder to stare in the face. I do not think that visiting your family home will do much to you other than show how far you have come in other ways. You are a successful businessman and that is in part due to your own hard work and diligence. You have a comfortable living you would not have experienced if you had not been given a veiled opportunity. You are smart and interesting and unlike any of the other men I have been acquainted with. I suppose in a way you have succeeded, it is up to you to decide if the cost was worth it'.

'Indeed I have lived comfortably these past ten years. I have wanted for nothing in terms of material items. I had a wife for a time that I grew to appreciate in many ways but there was always something missing. Always something I needed that she could not give. It was not that she did not please me in the bedroom or with her company. She did not understand me.....no one has ever understood me until I met you. I had never felt the urge to be with someone else, but when my eyes met yours for the first time something inside me melted and it is something that I cannot bear to lose. Yet I find that I would give up everything else that I have in my life......the money, the women and the house....all mean nothing. I often envisage what my life would be like if I had never left the farm. Perhaps I too would have been dead of fever ten years ago. Then again maybe I would be living here with a wife and children. Tending to the sheep and cows and just being able to pay the bills. My life may have been fuller with nothing than having everything and feeling empty'.

'Virgil just the same as you cannot change what is passed you cannot change our destinies. We have neither the resources nor the strength to fight what is coming. Take me down to this house of yours and let us see if we can at least ease some of your burden'.

We walk across the field until we come to the back yard. The gate that leads from the field is now hanging off its hinges due to neglect. It is as well there are no animals about to escape. Pushing it aside I walk through the gap and into the now overgrown yard. The weeds have taken over everything in sight they are even growing out the top of the cow tail pump. I fight my way through the brambles, nettles and everything else that has self seeded. Lifting the lid of the pump I look inside and discover a nest, all its inhabitants appear to have vacated, I remove it and the grass sticking around the lid. Checking the spout is now clear I pull the arm of the pump. It takes a few goes before the water starts to flow properly. I check the holes in the wall beside it and find that the old tin mug is still in its hiding place. I rinse it a few times and offer Lily some water. She takes it and then returning the mug I have some myself. It tastes different. The natural fresh water tastes so much better to that of the taps in Belfast.

'When I was a boy I used to run over the hills with the other lads and race down the slope to see who could get the tin mug first. Such innocence and all so that one of us would be the first to drink the spring water first. My mother would probably have been baking bread on the skillet or in the oven while my father looked after the animals. We had a simple life but we did not ever go hungry. This morning the smell of the bread frying in the house reminded me of my wedding breakfast and I felt a mixture of remorse and nausea combined with the anticipation of wanting to taste some fresh bread'.

'I have not often had the opportunity to bake. Most of my meals are made for me. On occasion when the masters have been absent the cook has shown me how to prepare dishes I have read about or liked. I am pretty good at making meals that I can combine with the herbs and spices I have read about in my books. Perhaps you will have the chance to try some of them while we are staying here'.

I nod my agreement. That would be nice, to sample her cooking and play at happy families for a time. I tramp down the nettles at the back entrance and push the lock on the door. It is stiff at first and I lean against the swollen damp wood with my shoulder. I push hard and the door moves a little. Eventually screeching open over the stoned floor of the kitchen.

The door has swollen with damp over the years and combined with birds and other animals having made their way into the house there is a build up of straw, dust, feathers and stones strewn across the floor. My mother would turn in her grave. She took such pride in keeping the house clean and the stone floor scrubbed. The wood pigeons and sparrows have evidently been nesting in the hearth and there are droppings and egg shells everywhere. The kitchen table that once was the heart and soul of the house is barely visible through the grime. I feel ashamed that I had not made an effort to come down and check out the house before. Looking around I remember all the happy times we spent huddled around the heat of the stove a bowl of broth in our hands and bread on the table. The woollen socks removed and heating on the cooker lid. While our toes turned from various shades of blue to pink. It was the hottest room in the house in the winter.

I can feel Lily's eyes watching me as I internalise my surroundings. She doesn't speak. I feel an overwhelming sense of sadness and fighting back the tears I walk to the foot of the wooden stairs. Tentatively I place my foot on the first rung checking that there isn't any woodworm. The boards creak with my weight but seem to be secure. Lily doesn't follow me. The sunlight is barely visible through the tattered curtain covering the window at the top of the stairs, yet it lets in enough light to see the dust dancing in the atmosphere.

The house is not large and above the kitchen there are two rooms. Three rooms in total for the privy is outside at the foot of the path. The room that I slept in for eighteen years is entered through the first door. It consisted of a small trunk bed and a blanket. The bed still lies as it was left when my parents died. Now covered in mouse droppings and eaten through by insects and vermin. I did not remember the room ever being as confined as I now find it to be. I feel claustrophobic at the thought that I can almost touch both walls with my arms if I were to stand in the middle of the room. There is also a distinct odour of neglect and mildew. My parents' room next door is not much bigger and their bed fills most of the space. A small set of drawers nestles behind the door. I look at it for a time before I decide to open the top drawer. I had never viewed the contents of my parents' drawers it was rude to pry and now I feel like I should leave them as I find them. Yet curiosity gets the better of me. I pull the first drawer open slowly and find it empty, and in the bottom there is nothing but old vests....... What did I expect after such a length of time? I suppose the minister and other locals had helped themselves to anything worth having. There was not much anyway for they had no fine jewellery or expensive belongings.

I have sinned greatly in my neglect of the house. It is all I have left to show of my lineage and the hard work my parents put in on a daily basis to keep a roof over our heads. They may not have had much but they had taken pride in keeping everything they had clean and tidy. If my mother could see the place now she would sit and weep. I feel a sudden urge to be sick, I have let them down yet again. I feel the acid build in my stomach and I run for the stairs. Straight down and out the back door I make it to the yard before my breakfast makes an unpleasant return.

My head spinning I retch until all I can taste is bile.

'Are you alright? Is there anything I can do to help?' Lily has appeared beside me and hands me the tin mug again full of water. I rinse my mouth and drink what is left in the mug. Sitting down on the stone wall at the side of the byre I rest my arms on my knees and breathe deeply to stop myself shaking.

It is some minutes before I reply to Lily who has stood silently watching me.

'I am fine now. I think the demons of the last ten years have just come back to haunt me all in one visit. Fear, shame, apprehension, sadness and my own naïve actions all here at once. I do not know what I should do to excise the past and I have no idea how I should be able to help you in the future. Where would I even begin? My parents cannot be here for me to beg for forgiveness, the house is in ruin and you......you are supposed to join my parents while I should be left to resemble the house, my life in ruins'.

'To begin with how about you visit your parents' grave. Surely seeing where they are resting will help a little. The house is not a ruin as such. Nothing a few days hard work wouldn't help put right. The rest....we have a few weeks left to determine'.

I am not used to being organised. She seems to have decided in a matter of seconds how I should help myself. I am more adept to getting my own way in most things, yet, I am also very good at burying my head in the sand. It is refreshing to have a clearer perspective on how I should proceed. Lily is of course correct; I am just feeling sorry for myself. Again I feel ashamed at my outburst. I am giving off about the state of a house when she has a death sentence hanging over her head. I know if it were my head I would probably be in a worse mental state than what I am in at present.

I walk to the pump and get myself some more water.

I return the mug to its resting place and turn to face Lily.

Resigned to the fact that she is indeed correct about how I should move forward I speak. 'I suppose you are right a trip to the graveyard would not be amiss. Sunday sermons should be long over by now and most people at their lunch. If we head in that direction we should hopefully avoid many of the local people a little while longer'.

The old graveyard can be reached by a narrow path just off the main road into the town. The grass path now resembles a hardened mud track due to the number of people who have traversed along it. This is a quicker route than walking further down and along the next road, then up the lane at the side of the church. We are taking the scenic route along the edge of the river and a small waterfall. If we visit the graves first then we will have time stop and admire the waterfall on the way back.

'Saint Patrick is supposed to have lived in a village on the edge of this river. He used the pool at the waterfall to baptise the villagers and those who followed his teachings. The graveyard itself is older than most imagine, there are records to prove it dates at least to the reformation. I think it is probably a lot older. We must walk passed the farm and then down a hill just after the apple orchard'.

'I have not been to an actual graveyard before. Any of the people who have died that I knew were removed. We presumed due to the nature of their deaths that they were never buried.......at least not formally'.

'I am sure you are right. When Emily and the child died they took her body away and disposed of it. I was not allowed to bury her as she had no official papers and her birth was never recorded. It is sad to think of people lying in paupers graves with no one to know if they are living or dead, no one to remember them or to tend their graves. I do believe it should be worse to be buried somewhere that no one should know about. In a forest, eaten by pigs or burned. Cast out with the refuge and disposed of in a worse fashion. This does of course happen and I turn a blind eye. I may have no family left to remember me but I do not want to lie forgotten in a ditch to be discovered in a hundred years by someone who has no hope of discovering who I have been'.

We pass the farm and I can smell the Sunday dinner through the open window. I feel hungry now that I no longer feel nauseous. Walking on we turn off to the right and down the stone path to the graveyard gate. The gate screeches open on its rusted metal joints. Not a large graveyard it is surrounded by a stone wall on three sides and a hedge on the side nearest the gate. The bottom left corner is home to a mort house from where the dead could be protected from grave diggers and thieves. Everywhere there are graves. In fact I am pretty sure that even under the sparse bits of grass that form the walkway there are more bodies. Littered with bodies the very colouration of the soil adds to my theory that this graveyard is indeed pre reformation. There are not many ornate graves but there are a lot of gravestones. My mother and father are buried somewhere near the gateway I presume as there is little space elsewhere.

I search the smaller headstones that are hidden in the undergrowth. Almost half way down the right hand wall I find their grave. A small circular shaped granite stone marks my parents resting place with just their names etched in the stone with the year of death. I mentally search my head for the bill the vicar had sent ten years previously and I am sure he has siphoned off a pretty penny for himself. The size of the stone does not equate to the amount of money I had posted to him.

Lily is standing at my side silently internalising my every action. She says nothing which I am now learning appears to be her way. I look at the stone and the dates and it gives me a sense that something has just ended. I look upward and over the stone wall. I turn and I look toward the bottom end of the enclosure. Everywhere I look I have a perfect view of the valley. In almost a one hundred and eighty degree motion I can see the hills and roads for almost twenty miles. This would indeed have been a fine place to hold a stand in the time of Robert the Bruce. An enemy could be spotted in every direction except from behind. The view gives me the sudden feeling of home sickness. This is however no longer my home. Those who made it home are resting beneath my feet and most of those I knew as a boy are dead or have moved elsewhere. This would not have happened before the famine and the fever at least not in such large numbers. Country folk would have lived in the same place their whole lives, looking after their land. Then when the turn came to take over the farm from parents they would all have lived under one roof and the next generation would take over the responsibilities, maybe ten or twelve people beneath one roof. Unfortunately the circumstances of latter years have meant a lot of locals had left the country behind them to move to the city or even go as far as Liverpool and Scotland. They have had to move to where they can make money to live.

It is such a good day there is hardly a cloud in the sky. This would be an ideal day for a war. Even it is only with my own demons. I breathe deeply and sigh. Everything has changed I can now only move forward and hope. I feel Lily touch my hand with hers and I hold it firmly. She still does not say anything but the simple gesture says more than what words could.

Standing in silence her hand in mine I realise that the simple gesture is having a more than simple effect on other parts of my anatomy and I feel warm, the heat having nothing to do with the cloudless weather. Absent minded I squeeze her hand a little tighter as my trousers become more constricted. Here surrounded by death I am still finding that I am unable to control my sinful urges. There seems to be many different types of darkness. The dark I fear and must always be smothered by and the darkness I am now living for the thoughts in the darkness of my now twisted mind. I must have an illness of the brain for as slow as they were to come all thoughts of my parents are now gone and all I can envisage is kissing Lily on the neck just above that repulsive maroon velvet. The colour does not suit her it makes her look as pale as a corpse. A very attractive corpse, one I would like to lie down on the ground between the gravestones and do all manner of sinful things with and to.

Lily is unaware of my thoughts as I watch her out of the corner of my eyes. I can see the swell of her breasts as she breaths, the slight parting of her lips and her eyes gazing into the distance. I imagine using my empty hand to cup her face, to lift her chin and to look into her eyes before kissing her……..claiming her as mine. My other hand releasing hers as I place it on her back pulling her closer, her tongue dancing with mine as I let her feel what she has done to me. Pulling her close to feel my hardness, I see myself lowering her to the earth and my hands feeling the curve of her legs as I raise her skirts. Then I slowly lower her under garments taking them off completely. I kiss the tips of her toes slowly, working my way up her leg, her stomach, her breasts, before again claiming her mouth as my own. I feel her hands on my buttocks and the desire in her as she pulls me closer. I use one hand to release my cock from my trousers. Then I gently spread her legs my hand finding the damp spot at the top. My fingers gently rub her clit and I feel her take a sharp intake of air as she is aware of new sensations. I gently slip one finger inside her and hear her moan.

'I need to feel you inside me. Don't make me wait any longer'. She whispers into my ear. The very sensation giving me goosebumps I raise myself up to enter her when she speaks again, this time in a very real voice distracting me from my lustful thoughts.

'How do you feel now? You have not said anything and I am unsure as to whether I should leave you to your reverie for a time'.

'You were indeed correct when you said that seeing the grave may help. This has been a form of catharsis and although I am not going to forget them I should have visited the grave sooner. Perhaps then my sense of guilt may not have been as great as it has become'.

How do I really feel now?

That I would lay you down surrounded by the echoes of the past, on the graves of the Godly and that I would wage war on my demons and yours. That with one look you can strip me bare and that in the house of the dead I would dance with you till dawn and never want it to end. That you can take me to hell for nothing is as it seems or as it should be. I feel that combined with the weather of a really glorious day that the touch of your hand has made me sin. My soul is on fire and I do not have the means or the mind to put out the flames.

'Perhaps we should head back. It has been a long morning and I am sure you are hungry. We have done enough soul searching for one day'.

She smiles and letting go of my hand she leads the way out of the graveyard. I take one final look at the gravestone and follow her. I close the gate behind us. Noting that the only sign we had been there was the print of our feet in the mossy ground.

I would really have liked to look at the waterfall on the way back but it is late afternoon now and it will take us a while walking back to the house. It will be teatime before we get there. It is best that we leave it for another day. Tomorrow is the start of a new week and we shall start it by sorting out some new clothes for Lily.

We walk the length of the street and I can see that the blue shop in the middle of the thoroughfare is still doing a trade. The mops and buckets are sitting in the street ready for the potential customer to come along and purchase them, while the window is filled with different types of materials. I cannot see the name of the shop from the angle I am walking but on approach I see that it is no longer owned by Mr and Mrs Fox. It is simply called 'The Blue Room'. I tell Lily that before I moved to Belfast I used to work in this shop and was very good at my job. The fact that I was good at it was not a good thing as it drew the attention of Mr Samuel McAuley who then set his mind on adding me to 'The Order of the Dragons'. I am curious as to what has happened Mr. Fox as he was not old enough to be retired. It is maybe a good thing that the owners will not have any knowledge of me so that they do not ask too many questions I will not be willing to answer.

The old familiar sound of a high pitch bell chimes as we push open the front door and enter the shop. It has been a while since I had been to purchase the material for making clothes and the smell of the new linen and flax material mixed with the dyes and preservatives fills my nostrils. The mix of smells can be quite intoxicating at this side of the counter. In the store I can remember it could be rather toxic at times. Nowadays not all the material is dyed at the shop. Large factories can produce larger quantities of already coloured linen, cotton, velvet or silk. This means that the more toxic of chemicals do not need used in the vicinity of customers. The large beetling mills around these parts still function in part but are not employing as many people as they were used to in the past.

Immediately a young girl possibly no more than thirteen appears from the back store. She is rather small with a stoop in her back despite her young age, I presume that she has been sewing for a number of years and the bending over material and stitching has caused this unfortunate deformity. Her hands red raw from working with water and chemicals and her apron far from being starched white looks like it has never seen a wash. I make the assumption that the new owners are not as pernickety and fastidious about their work. Despite the girls obvious inflictions she greets us with a smile and a polite, 'How can I be of service?'

'Would the proprietor be available to discuss some business this morning?' I ask.

'No sir, he normally does not appear until after luncheon his wife is here though if that would be of help?'

'If your mistress could help us that would indeed be useful'.

She moves slowly my mother would have said 'like the dead lice were dropping off her'. I can hear her open the back door into the adjoining yard and gulder, 'Mrs, you've got some posh gent asking to speak to you'.

Lily and I stand in awkward silence looking at the girl who has returned to keep and eye on us while we wait. Some five minutes later the door in the store closes and the lady appears. The last person I expected to see was Mrs. Fox standing there in the doorway, as smart as the girl was through other. She recognises me at once and coming around to the other side of the counter she hugs me and takes a good look at myself and Lily before declaring that we are both a sight for sore eyes.

'Virgil, what have you been doing with yourself these last few years? I have not clapped eyes on you since you left for the big smoke...... before the fever....I was sorry to hear that your parents had died. Mr. Fox and I survived the local outbreak despite our close contact with almost everyone. Constitution of old boots we had. He managed to survive that only to get kicked in the head by a horse while walking down to the new dining rooms. He walked out that door to meet Mr. McAuley and five minutes later he was dead. Mr. McAuley had witnessed the whole thing and was distraught. He offered to pay for the funeral services and expenses. They had come to know each other well over the years and knowing he could afford the cost I did not refuse'.

I assume that Mr. Fox's death was not an accident and that the offer of payment was the workings of a guilty conscience. She stops for breath and I judge this as my opportunity to take over the conversation while I have the chance.

'I am sorry to hear of Mr. Fox's death I had hoped that he may be able to make some new clothes for my ward. She has recently been placed under my care and does not appear to have much suitable attire. I could of course have made them myself but I am at present very busy with other matters. Would you be able to undertake the task yourself?' I look over at the girl as if to imply that I do not want the girl working on the clothes.

'The girl certainly does not have your skill Virgil and as you can see she is not as clean. She does however work hard despite an appearance to the contrary. My new husband he keeps to himself and does very little of anything, unfortunately so I should be glad of the custom. I shall be sure to undertake all the stitching myself. What do you require?'

'Lily here has no clothes with her at all for dinner parties, day wear or housewear. I would like her fitted for around six changes of clothes to begin with. I would also like her to have a 'sheeles green' velvet dress with a red velvet cloak. Shoes, under garments and accessories will also be needed for each outfit. Lily can choose the material and style of the outfits herself. If you could measure her today and make all the decisions would it be possible to have them all ready in about four days?'

'I will do my best Virgil if we get all the measurements and material sorted the main task will be the stitching. My eyes are not what they used to be so using the candle at night is troublesome. If I get Joanne to do some of the inside stitching it would be quicker'.

Mrs. Fox, as I shall probably always refer to her now, looks at me questioningly to make sure that it is suitable for the arrangement she just suggested. I nod my agreement and remark 'if you feel that is the best course of action then I shall leave it in your capable hands'.

She flusters about pulling out the rolls of the most expensive material that are in stock Normally I would have been disgusted with the greedy nature but I forget I probably look like a rich gentleman to her now, someone who can afford the better material. The assumption is correct so I suppose I should not begrudge her a good sale after all she will be working hard to earn her shillings. I remember the hours taken cutting the cloth measuring the edges and tacking my material before I could even begin to stitch the pieces into their correct places. I have grown lazy; now, I draw the designs as required by the rich gentlemen for their lady slaves and often direct someone else to put everything together. I no longer have any interest in making the clothes myself. Perhaps I should change that; it would be a better way to fill my days than sitting drinking myself into depressed submission.

Mrs. Fox brings out the measuring tape and takes all Lily's dimensions. She then shows her the materials. I am not entirely sure I like the colours. It takes a certain colour of cloth to bring out the colour of redhair.

'Perhaps blue or crimson or rustic colours would suit better', I suggest.

Mrs. Fox indicates to the girl to hand her different material, thicker in quality but not as expensive. I can see her frown. The colours are however a better match and I indicate for them to proceed. She also looks out some cream linen and silk material for under garments and petticoats.

Lily having remained silent until now states, 'I do not need so many underclothes I feel I should suffocate if had so much material on top of my corsets'.

Mrs. Fox doesn't seem to approve and looks at me for agreement before proceeding.

'Whatever Lily wants Mrs. Fox we shall do that'.

They proceed to pick a few more colours and material. Then move onto a choice of accessories. It takes a good hour or so to get the materials, measurements and oddments all within a workable order. I watch and I wait and say very little more. When they are concluded Lily and I take our leave and promise to call back at the end of the week.

'You are more than generous Virgil. I shall not need so many clothes'.

'My dear, you shall have whatever you want. I would however prefer that you have something a little less distracting than you are wearing at present. You shall have plenty of opportunity to wear your new attire. Let us cross over to the other side of the road. The Central Dining Room should have something suitable for us to eat before we return home'.

I offer her my arm and escort her across to the stone built establishment at the opposite side. Pushing open the glass fronted door we enter to the smell of baking. We make ourselves comfortable at the only available table and wait to be served. I order stew as it has been a while since I had some that resembled good country food. Lily chooses the vegetable broth, not that there was really much choice but the food will fill a hole until we dine this evening.

When the food arrives with both eat in relative silence. This is partially due to the ruckus being created by the other patrons who despite the early hour appear to have had a few drinks. The food however is very tasty and the best I have tasted in a long while. I am not very good at cooking for myself, mostly due to laziness or sheer mental exhaustion.

Lily speaks over the droning noise, 'I should like to try and make some stew some night. You know on the continent they add all sorts of different herbs and spices to make it taste more interesting. Is there somewhere we can get some herbs?'

'I am sure there is wild parsley, thyme, rosemary and a few other things growing about in the fields. I am not to sure about spices. I think they are still rather expensive to purchase. I shall ask the cook when we return to the house.....or perhaps you could do that yourself as I may not ask the correct questions. If you like when can take the long way back and check the fields for the other herbs'.

'Yes it would be nice to see a different view on the way back. I am sure we can see a lot more of the landscape on the descending journey. Did you never collect parsley or thyme before when you were small?'

We start walking back towards the fields.

'No my mother never really used anything other than maybe pepper for seasoning. We only ever had salt when someone brought us some on the sly from Carrickfergus salt mines. It is still rather expensive. Even now my salt dish is small. I am not as rich as some of the other gentlemen in the order or indeed in my banking acquaintance who would have salt boats or large dishes on their tables. I do know there should be some parsley in the third field across from the house. The rest we shall just have to search harder to find'.

We find parsley in a few fields and Lily picks a few other yellow coloured plants that she says are useful for dyeing. Enough that should keep her going for a few days, should she decide to give the cook a hand in the kitchen.

I awaken to find myself enshrined in a tomb of bed linen my limbs bound in a tangled mess. I had slept well but I must have been restless in my unconscious state. I unravel myself from my bed clothes and throw the linen aside as I rise to sit on the edge of the bed. There is a chill in the air and I presume it must be earlier than I expect. Walking across to the opposite side of the room on tip toes across the cold wood floor I check the clock to find it is only six o clock. It is bright outside. I suppose in Belfast surrounded by all the large buildings I find that the sun does not appear to rise as early; at least it appears that way because the buildings cast shadows keeping out the light. I go downstairs dressed as I am and ask for some water to wash. When I have washed myself and shaved I get dressed. I then knock on Lily's bedroom door I do not receive a reply. Pushing the door ajar slightly on squeaky hinges I look in to find she is still asleep. I close the door gently again and go down for breakfast.

Looking out the window to the garden and the fields beyond I suddenly have the urge for some fresh duck eggs. When I was little I used to go to the river bank and collect the eggs so mother could boil them or bake with them. If I go out now the ducks should be up out of their nests and I would be back before half eight.

Despite that it is now the month of June it is chilly and damp outside the morning dew still hanging in the air. I return to the house and put on an overcoat. Climbing the stile at the bottom of the garden I notice that I have left footprints in the wet grass. I enter the field at the bottom of the estate and wander through the cattle and head for the main road. Although the estate is large there is as far as I know no access to the river bank or ponds. Crossing the road I head up the hill towards the church branching off at a small forest of trees. Anyone who did not know this area would not know that the façade of oaks and birches hides a small enclosed lake surrounded by a small mountain of granite. It is just as I remember it being perhaps a little more over grown the water reeds protruding from the marshy bank and larger ones sticking out of the water at the centre of the lake. 'My ladies lace' is growing in clumps around the tree edges and creeping towards the water. This used to be a great spot for ducks. They would lay their eggs in the shorter reeds just at the dry land hidden from the eyes of predators.

I head towards the waters edge only to realise that I am now a lot heavier and I sink in the muddy ground around the reeds. Almost losing my boot I pull my foot from the ground which is now trying to devour me. I stand and think for a moment before deciding to remove my boots and socks and roll my trousers up to my knees. Perhaps not the most sensible of plans but I am hoping the ground will not move as much under my weight, that I may sink from view.

I also remove my outer coat and head again towards the reeds. They are hard under my feet and it is not an entirely pleasant experience. I step on the reeds rather than the ground between them as I feel it to be more solid than the land. Lifting the reeds and grass aside I search for the duck eggs. After a few minutes searching I come across a small stash, three eggs hidden nicely under the shadow of a larger group of reeds. I lift them gently, only then realising that I have not brought anything in which to carry them. I have come on this errand virtually unprepared. In the old days I would have had a bag and remembered that I would have to remove my shoes. Years of living in the town have numbed my mind to being prepared for the smaller details of living.

I wade back to the firmer ground my feet caked in mud and slime. I place the eggs on my coat and do my best to clean my feet on the grass before replacing my socks and boots. I remember the summer days I would have sat here with a small fishing line drifting in and out of a dreamworld trying to catch an eel or some river trout. I didn't often catch anything much worth keeping. There were plenty of sticklebacks to be found but sure they weren't even a mouthful. I could have probably have eaten them alive for all they would have filled my stomach. Those were the days of no worry and the days I hoped my dreams would come true, innocent dreams of fancy houses, horses and the odd flaxen haired farmer's daughter. Now my dreams take a darker twist and I am scared of what I dream for fear they do actually come true.

Placing an egg in each pocket of my coat and holding the third I begin to walk back to the big house. I walk through the copse of trees and out the other side. Many more people are up now; I can see the smoke exiting the chimneys of the occasional house on the horizon. I stop and breathe in the clean country air. Adding an inch to my step I walk back down the hill in squelching socks thinking about my handpicked boiled eggs.

On entering the scullery through the tradesman's entrance on account of my squelching feet, I remove my socks and shoes. Then tip toe to the sink with the eggs, not because I don't want to be heard but because the stone floor is freezing. Then I remember I will need water from the outside pump to wash the dung and feathers from the eggs. Hoping cook might do this for me, now I've taken my shoes off, I leave the eggs on the sideboard and tip toe through the pantry to the hallway. Then straight up the servants stairs two at a time to change my trousers and socks. Excited over the prospect of my breakfast I don't linger. It's a very little thing but I feel smug that I collected my own food for the first time in years. Now presentable, in 'gentleman's terms', I take the front stairs down to the dining room. I walk through to the kitchen to find the cook is now returned and has already washed the eggs.

I feel such a fraud asking her to prepare them for me but I have become accustomed to living 'like the other half' live. It won't last forever and I may as well make the most of it while I can.

While waiting for my breakfast I check if there has been any mail. A few letters and cards are waiting on the Mahogany sideboard. The cards do not seem to be anyone I know and are probably from some nosey gentleman neighbours wanting to see if they can marry their daughters off to someone with money and standing.

I have neither, so they are out of luck.

The letters are mostly addressed to Mr. McAuley with the exception of one with a familiar red seal. Immediately my stomach enters my mouth and I dread breaking the wax to read the contents.

Staring at the cream manuscript for a time I take a deep breath and use the knife on the table to cut the envelope open. Dropping the knife immediately, as if it burnt me, I have a sensation that the knife could have been used for something other than cutting food. It is amazing how unsettling the simple sight of a symbol can be on nerves. Hands now trembling visibly I remove the single sheet of card and read:

No name. the correspondence states.

Dear member, your company shall be expected at a soiree to be held at your residence on this Saturday evening 12th June 1858. Servants have already been informed. The Master of the house shall not be in attendance as he shall not be required for our upcoming event, we expect you to entertain the guests. Some will arrive from midday but none will stay the night. Perhaps your house guest can entertain the wives while you discuss business with the men.

The Order

That will be in four days time. I need to talk to Lily and prepare her for what is expected of her. Mrs. Fox had better have those clothes ready for Friday. I mull everything over in my head. There isn't any point going into town today but tomorrow is market day. We shall go in and check on the progress of the dresses and see what food there is at the stalls.

Four days.
Dread.
Fear.
Uncertainty.

Words, they are everything and yet nothing. They open doors, light paths, create darkness and cut to the heart. Endless connections, connotations, links, grouped together to create a kaleidoscope of patterns, sentences, stories, memories, things of beauty that can make even the prettiest of mouths ugly or evil.

Words ruminate in the memory they create a foundation for our thoughts and feelings. Yet often people use them without thought or discernment. They tell use one thing yet it means another. Even the whitest of sheep can provide clothing for a wolf. One that creeps up over time to sink in its teeth but is unaware that you knew it was coming. The subtle change innate in every person, their sensibilities, their monogram or trademark, everyone uses words differently it's like a thumb print; that one word that slips into a conversation that doesn't fit the pattern an indelible mark in your mind. One word that can create doubt, fear, despair, its implications greater than any demon hiding under your bed. That one word, 'Order'.

I'm not entirely sure why, but I feel like I should have to pack an entire lifetime into four days. The uncertainty of not knowing what may happen, who will be there, what they will do, what they will do with........her. I feel the need to make every second count. Four days in her company will seem like minutes and I know I should want hours, days.....years.

I hear footsteps approaching from the kitchen and hide the letter under the rest of the pile. My Ulster breakfast of bacon, boiled eggs and wheaten farls arrives on the table. I think I have well earned this food as I retrieve the knife from the carpet and with trembling hands begin to eat.

The morning is again dry and the walk into town is pleasant, it does not take us long to dander the distance. The street is busier than it had been on Monday. It is lined with stalls laid out on the back of old wooden barrow carts. Men and women selling their wares of fruit and vegetables, saddles, the tanner selling also some fine leather gloves and muffs. I tell Lily to watch where she is standing as the cobbles are also littered with manure from the various animals that are to be sold at the auction. Further up there is a cart selling all manner of colours of ribbon and spools of cotton and thread. Lily is immediately attracted to the palette of colours and we purchase a quantity in different shades.

There are also dealers of every possible household item or curiosity, the wealth of ages piled high for all to see. Many of which may be found in some of the finer pawnbrokers in Belfast. They may or may not have been acquired legally but the price will reflect a quick sale in most cases. Having said that the prices seem to fluctuate according to the customers dress and whether they look like they have money. Some of the richer farmers often take to wearing their older clothes when attending the market as it makes the sellers think they are not as well off. Meaning they often get a bargain on their purchases. Like chameleons they blend into their surroundings and if they have been able to barter they know they have at least got the best deal they can muster.

When we draw parallel with the Tailors shop we enter and the girl is again at the counter. Obviously having recognised us from the previous occasion she again lets out a gulder for Mrs. Fox, who after several minutes awkward silence appears in the doorway.

'Good morning Virgil, I hope you aren't here expecting your dresses to be ready today', although she laughs her eyes do not reflect the mirth.

'Mrs. Fox, we are not here to collect today but I have just been made aware of an engagement at the weekend and would require that they would definitely be ready for Friday evening at the latest'.

She gives me a withering look and then looks at Lily and back to me.

'Virgil you know the work which goes into these clothes it may mean I need to take on another girl for a few days just to get the hemming and collars complete'.

I am aware she now smells the banker's drafts and the clink of a few sovereigns.

I ensure her that the extra help would not be a problem and that she should bill me accordingly. We shall however be over no later than four o clock on Friday.

'I hope that you have a good day Mrs Fox, the market should ideally bring you a few more customers'.

Turning to leave I half forgot that Lily was with me as she had been silently observing up until now.

Lily addresses Mrs Fox.

'Before we leave, I was just wondering if you would have a small bottle of Sheeles Green? I have had a fancy to making some blancmange and jelly'.

Mrs. Fox scratches her head a second and then looks to the ceiling as if she has forgotten something. Her eyebrows nearly meeting in the middle, not that they actually don't already meet, she turns and heads back through the doorway returning a few moments later with a small brown bottle.

'There's a new bottle she says as she hands it to Lily. We don't really use it all that much anymore. Make sure you don't add too much to whatever you are making just a few drops is enough to provide a little colour'.

Handing the bottle to Lily she looks at me.

'I'll add it to the bill'.

Nodding agreement I once more bid her anon and hold the door open for Lily. Doffing my hat to Mrs Fox I exit the shop.

Now that we have attended to the chief purpose of coming to town we can at least browse the rest of the stalls at our leisure.

It is amazing how much stuff seems to come off something as limited in space as a small horse cart. Once spread out it seems to take up quite a bit of space compared to when it is all compactly packed on top of each other on the cart. There are various other carts and stalls which are of some interest containing a good amount of curiosities, various different vanity items and those which appear oriental in origin.

A dagger with a serrated blade, surrounded by a gilded silver handle and the shape of a baphomet protruding out of the top is very different I am surprised that the tinker who is selling it has not been lynched by the local Presbyterians already. It is very unusual and I am in two minds whether I should buy it.

'How much is the knife?' I ask the man. He has swarthy skin that looks as if it has been well leathered and in need of a good wash. I presume he spends a lot of time out of doors. I doubt that the dagger would make much impression on him as he looks to be fairly thick skinned both in his manner and his composition. Although in reality it would probably make him bleed as much as any other man.

In a rather southern brogue he responds, 'Sir, for you just one guinea, you couldn't say much better than that. Where else would you be getting an item as odd and rare as this?' he takes it from me and rubs the tip of his finger up the serrated edge before placing the tip under my chin. 'It's cut price that's for sure', he states with a twinkle in his eye at his little joke. 'I'll even wrap it for you', he removes it from my chin and places it in a rough sack he has sitting under the leg of an old stool. 'Definitely better than a pig in a poke'. With that he places the sack in my hand keeping hold of one end and holds out his other hand for payment, before I know what I am doing I've handed him a guinea and he's handed me the knife and my minds been made up for me. One guinea lighter and a heavier with the weight of a dagger; I have no purpose for, save for its novelty value.

While I have been railroaded into my purchase Lily has been perusing the items on the next stall. She's holding a very unusual mirror item. Looking over her shoulder I see it is circular in base very similar to the compasses found on ships with a flat surface. The mirror itself is dark almost black in colour showing a sign of age. Looking into it I can almost see the sea and a certain eerie depth to the reflection.

Taking the item from Lily I notice it is covered in engraved markings, the base is of a texture that appears to be pinchbeck although it is the most exquisite finishing in such i've seen, despite the strange mirror. They are almost like the pictures of hieroglyphs which I had seen in some periodicals. Another very unusual item! Lily appears fascinated by it........

'Would you like it?' I ask.

'What use have I for such items, in a few more days I shall have no need to know what I look like. Looking into it though is like looking at your soul, it is so very dark; Look into my eyes and all you will see, every part of my soul displayed, that's me. A cloudy gaze, I'm miles away, Sorry what was that you say? A smile, a frown, on my lips you see, But you know that's not all of me. From the fire and passion, sadness and disaster, perhaps I have little time for laughter, Look into my eyes, listen......don't hear. Can you tell the real me my dear?'

Lily looks at me as if she is asking me that question, can I see the real her, her soul, not just that what she wants others to see in her eyes.

I smile. I do not need a mirror to see her soul.

'That's what is called a 'moon mirror'; the man selling the mirror suddenly chips in.

'It supposedly has supernatural properties. I've no clue why it's called a moon mirror though, I've tried to reflect it in it several times and it never shows. It supposedly belonged to one of the witches up at Islandmagee; at least that is what I am told'.

'Perhaps it is called after the moon because when placed on a flat surface the mirror is facing the sky. During the day it would reflect the light and brighten a room and at night as there is not so much light it should reflect the moon in full, although as you say with the mirror being so black that may not be possible, and you would need to be outside or in a glass house', Lily hypothesises.

'You could be right Mrs., indeed you could, and where else would you find one?' he smells the anticipation of a sale, and looks at Lily with one eyebrow raised knowingly waiting to take our money.

Purchasing the item off the man I hand it to Lily to place in the satchel she is carrying. I also hand her the knife which she takes and quizzically feels through the sack. Then she briefly looks up at me with a strange look in her eyes. The look in her eyes gone as quickly as it arrived as if hidden behind a shutter.

'Would you like to go to the 'Dining Rooms' again? Or shall we head back to the 'big house?'

I hadn't called it that since we arrived I find it strange that I refer to it as the 'big house' now. Perhaps it is just all the familiarity of home starting to seep back into my head.......or is it the familiar sense of foreboding returning?

'Let's just return to the house Virgil it's been an interesting morning but I think I should like to return to the familiar surroundings and maybe try some cooking myself while cook is still working'.

We begin to walk back through the cobbled manure covered street and out to the fields. There are not many folk about on the return journey and we cross the fields relatively quickly.

Yesterday was a fairly quiet day but I find that I am still exhausted when I wake up. It must be the country air and the long walks, something I am no longer used to, making me tired. I turn over on my side and wrap my hands around the feather bolster to plump it up under my head. I dread the prospect of getting up today and I am not entirely sure whether it is through a general foreboding or general malaise. Throwing the covers from the top of me I lie a few more minutes before pushing myself up and placing my feet on the floor. It is cold this morning and I feel a chill through my nightshirt. If I didn't need to urinate badly I think my clothes would have been pulled on in double quick time. Instead I use the chamber pot and wish the fire in my room was lit. It feels like autumn instead of almost summer.

I go down to breakfast to find that Lily has already eaten and is helping cook in the kitchen. I wonder what the fascination is with the scullery? If I were in her shoes I would be doing anything but cooking especially when there is someone already there to do it for me. Instead Lily is standing pulling the feathers off what appears to be a partridge or a pigeon the white and gray feathers floating aimlessly before drifting to a halt, more around than in the box in which Lily is placing them.

Backing slowly out the door I leave before I get asked to help.

Although we had walked through the garden several times now I had not really stopped to admire the different colours and shapes, although not too extravagant in its design is very well kept with a host of topiary artwork and a lot of colourful flowers. It is more in keeping with the English countryside than that of a European Grand Tour.

I think about the night I met Lily just a few days ago and how I thought her parents were avid botanists. Her name really does loan itself to someone who is very keen on flowers or maybe poetry. Roses are often the topic of poems, songs, sonnets or verse. They are frequently likened to a woman. Turning towards the light and away from the darkness the rose bud grows and blossoms until it reaches maturity, like the blossoming cheeks of a girl, rose coloured lips as 'the coquet blushes as she shyly looks from under flickering eyelashes'. These are all on the surface purely cosmetic facades to an inner beauty or the roses scent. Flowers are plucked while in their full bloom and in poetry this refers to a woman being fucked or taken in her prime. Once a rose is plucked unless it is nurtured and fed it begins to die. If you have ever observed this you will have noticed that unlike many other genus of flowers. The rose withers and decays from the inside out, its colour fading gradually from the stem, to the edge of its petals. *Should you be compared to a red red rose?* The fledging bud unless attended to often or groomed shall no longer grow, a bit like a girl with a broken heart. Like the rose the heart dies from within and the sorrow spreads like a disease to the outer appearance, strangled by the thorny hold of grief. While there is a facade to hide behind in a person this may not always be evident as some become accustomed to hiding behind the outward appearance.

Rose is the bud about to be plucked and she is doing a very good job of hiding behind her facade.

Plucking a bunch of roses, orange lilies and foxglove I take them in to the dining room and finding a vase set them in the centre of the table. Then I disappear to the library for a time to keep myself occupied.

Some hours later I hear the gong for the dining room being battered. I presume Lily is summoning me for my dinner.

Entering the room I find the table laid out for us both with food set out in tureens. Normally we would just eat what cook has made but today Lily seems to have made us a banquet.

'You have been busy, for someone who has never cooked before?'

'Cook showed me what to do; we have a couple of appetisers, a main meal and dessert. Something a little different, I hope you like them. To begin assorted wild mushrooms and dandelion soup made from the smoked roots, followed by Pigeon in comport sauce with parsley, carrots and potatoes, then for afters mint jelly in chocolate sauce. We also have dandelion and burdock wine or plum and apple. I thought I would try out some ideas and maybe use them at the 'last supper''.

'Cook will be here and I'm sure help has been arranged for her for that evening. They will not want you to be cooking. You will be the guest of honour. This looks very interesting though I have not ever had dandelion soup before or mint jelly'.

The dandelion soup is a little sour and tastes of burnt charcoal which I am sure it is not supposed to, but I say nothing. The taste of the mushrooms disguises much of the after taste. I am not sure they are all types of mushrooms I have had before either, 'Where did you pick the mushrooms?'

'I didn't cook had already them sitting in the kitchen I just chopped them and added butter. Do you not like them?'

'I was just curious I don't want to be dropping over dead in a moment from a poisonous one'.

Lily gives me a strange look. Thinking nothing of it I pour us both a glass of the apple and plum wine as I don't think I can face any more dandelions. Taking a drink I wash away the strange tastes. Surely the pigeon cannot have gone wrong so I carve us both a couple of slices and add the vegetables. Lily keeps looking at me intently I can tell she wants to know she has made a good attempt. Through a full mouth of pigeon I try to tell her it is really tasty. The pigeon does taste better and I'm sure cook had more of a hand in its preparation. Pouring another glass of wine I eat the rest of the main meal. The wine must be pretty strong as are most homemade concoctions because I start to feel like I'm very well oiled before reaching the bottom of the second glass. Lily on the other hand has not finished the first glass and has poured herself some water. I follow her example and pour myself a glass of water also and do my best to appear sober with shaking hands.

'Are you feeling well Virgil? You are rather flushed'.

I assure her I am fine that the homemade brew appears to have gone straight to my head and that the jelly and sauce will help sober me up. Although I am not as convinced now as the room is starting to spin slowly.

Lily serves me a portion of the jelly from the copper mould and pours some of the chocolate sauce over the top, a delightful combination of hot and cold. In the hope that the sugar content will make me feel better I have it eaten in a few bites. She has not even had time to serve her own. Feeling a little rude that I have eaten so fast I pour another glass of water. I now feel very thirsty and disorientated.

I can just about make out Lily asking me if I am ill again, her voice sounding like it is on a gramophone with a broken needle, very deep and elongated something like imagine the voice of the devil may sound. I know I am looking at her like she has grown a set of horns but I cannot stop myself. It is as if there is a halo of fire around her head and her eyes are red as coals. I am not convinced that I am well now nothing like this has ever happened before when I have been drunk, that wine must be nearly as potent as poteen. I'd always heard men say it was strong enough to blind a man.

Lily comes closer or what I thought was her the eyes burning a hole right through my skin I put my hands up to protect myself from the fire, brushing at my arms as if to brush away the flames from my body. Pushing her aside I pour the water over my arms, I've got to put it out.......looking back at Lily I cannot see her in her place is a tall black demon with red eyes and breathing fire.

Where has Lily gone? What has it done with her?

'Lily, Lily where are you?' I scream hearing no reply but the gramophone like sounds from the devil I run from the room.

Where will I hide? Inside, outside, the kitchen, the library, can't go to the library it'll burn the books, outside to the pond it can't burn me in the water.

I no longer recognise my surroundings, everything is vague, unclear, drifting in and out of a sea of white mist, all my surroundings appear distant. Standing, my carver chair falls behind me. Pushed backwards with some force the legs scrape the stone floor, my legs flailing wildly, avoiding the flames as they lick my body with an essence of urgency.

All the while the voice continues, 'Lily, Lily!'

I am no longer sure to whom the voice belongs; it draws out the syllables of her name with an excessive longing.

Is it my voice?

Is it that of the devil?

Is it some other invisible force?

Reaching the hall I follow the contours of the wall, slowly groping my way along the red velvet walls, pulling my way along the folds and frills, in and out hiding between the brass oil lamps. They are not lit, yet it is dark.....what time of day is it?

My feet like lumps of lead move slowly beneath me, the door is in sight. Leaving the security of the red velvet folds I reach out to the light.

11th June 1858

Waking from the mist I sit upright with a start, my heart thumping in my chest and ringing in my ears. I immediately check for the flames, my arms flapping. Quickly I realise I am not on fire, in the pond, or nearly dead, as I register the crumpled mass of linen sheets in front of me.

I see Lily watching me from the confines of a dark green leather wingback chair. A glimmer of daylight escapes through the drapes across her face, the dust particles making it appear as if she is shimmering in light. She does not move. She just stares at me as if taking in my every action, or maybe I should say reaction, for it feels like she is studying me like a scientist.

Absently I run my hand through my wayward hair. I imagine I resemble someone who has had a fight with a whin bush and lost. My mouth is dry and I feel slightly nauseous. I feel like I should have consumed a vast quantity of alcohol, yet I am sure I had very little.

Swinging my legs around to the edge of the bed slowly at the rate of an eighty year old man with arthritic joints, the room spins and I know I need a lot of water.

Lily moves from her position of solitude and pours a glass of water from a decanter sitting on a side of drawers.

Handing me the glass I grab hold of her wrist and look at her face. She cannot look at me.......and I wonder why that should be the case. Perhaps I frightened her with my actions, heaven knows I scared myself. I take the glass from her and drink without voicing my thoughts.

She takes the glass off me and refills it before asking, 'How do you feel? You gave me quite a fright, one minute you were eating and the next running around as if possessed before you collapsed in the hallway'.

'How did I get to bed?'

'The servants carried you upstairs, I was not entirely sure you should be left alone, so I've been watching and waiting for you to wake up. Perhaps I should stay out of the kitchen and leave it to the experts in future? I will get cook to make breakfast. We have a lot to do today'.

Lily leaves the room and I am still disorientated. Ringing the servant's bell I ask that a bath be brought up and set before the fire. Shivering slightly I ask that the fire be lit. I am sure I have not felt this bad with the effects of the night before since the first night I had a drink. By the time I nibble at the fried breakfast and washed I feel almost human again. Still slightly green but it is now bearable.

Lily arrives back in the room dressed to go out. It has completely left my head that we are supposed to go into town to collect her dresses. We should probably take the carriage as the clothes will be quite heavy to carry and I don't think I have the energy to trail over the fields with dresses and corsets.

Sometime later having had to fetch the horses and get them ready we are on our way. Trotting along at a steady speed it will be a short journey today......and for that I am grateful.

Mrs. Fox is at the counter when we arrive almost as if she had been anticipating our arrival, or perhaps she smelt the money she would hopefully be receiving. The garments appear to be already wrapped and lying on top the broad wooden platform in brown paper.

'Good morning, Mrs. Fox, how are you today. I presume that everything is ready?'

'Indeed Virgil. All ready to go', she pats the pile of wrapped materials.

I am only too aware that they may not be correctly finished, or fit. I suggest that Lily may try each outfit on now as I do not want to have to come back at another point in time.

Mrs. Fox does not appear pleased but ushers Lily into the tailoring room. Closing the door behind her although not entirely shut, as the door has swollen with damp.

I look at the floor and brush the toe of my shoe on the back of my trousers to make it shine. I cannot make out much conversation but I can see just about through a gap in the door. Mrs. Fox is pulling the lace stays in a blue corset, tight on Lily's back. If she was any rougher she may as well place Lily face down on the ground and use her feet for added force.

They emerge a good half hour later, both happy that all the outfits are a satisfactorily finished.

I hand Mrs. Fox's outstretched hand a handful of bank notes and guineas. She smiles like a Cheshire cat and says, 'Health to wear', before opening the door for us and ushering us into the street'.

'Thank you, Mrs. Fox for your hard work hopefully Lily will indeed get good wear out of your creations'.

Hearing the shop bell ring behind us as the door shuts, I usher Lily to the cart which is standing in the street opposite. Placing the clothing between us, I help Lily into the carriage before heading back towards the house.

On returning I find a letter has arrived in our absence.

Dear Sir,
The girl shall be collected tomorrow morning to spend the day with some of the members' wives. They will not be aware of who she is so please inform her to introduce herself as your ward, and that she was the daughter of one of your

cousins. This will allow the extra servants to prepare the house and the food for the rest of the members.

Your ward shall be returned with the other ladies once we have eaten. Sometimes it is best to keep up appearances and act like every other gentleman's club.

We shall discuss arrangements for the solstice feast tomorrow.

Your fellow Dragon

I inform Lily of the arrangements at dinner that evening and that she should take the clothes she is to wear with her in the morning. I am sure she knows how to behave but the etiquette of someone who lives mostly alone may not always be up to public standards or rather stand up to public ridicule.

'Virgil! I shall behave! If you recall I met you at a public evening, after last night antics it is I who should be telling you to behave accordingly!'

Feeling reprimanded I nod in agreement. Perhaps she is right, an early night is in order so both of us have our nerves and wits about us tomorrow.

The Moon

A tarot card of fertile imagery and female characteristics the moon provides us with a myriad of emotions and possibilities; a card of darkness and uncertainty with many connotations a sign of unstable moods, hope but also confusion. The different phases of the moon can provide different meanings to various groups, such as farmers, pagans, witches to name a few. Every twenty nine and a half days the moon disappears, it hides from the earth then emerges from its shadow, it again vanishes and the whole cycle starts again. This in some religions is seen as the birth and death of the moon. The word 'moon' comes from the Greek word 'to measure'. Each phase of the moon has its own significance and effects on emotions, planting, crops, fertility and the rise and fall of the tides. Witches believe that different phases of the moon have different effects on their spells.

A new moon or crescent shaped moon as seen in the tarot is a sign of new beginnings and opportunities while the waxing moon is a sign of growth in relationships, finance or learning. It is often thought that this is the perfect time for fertility and pregnancy. The waxing moon is also a time for communication and healing. The Full moon, when the moon is at its greatest size is a time of enlightenment and heightened psychic awareness. This is the ideal time for ideas and commitment while the waning moon is a time for banishment rituals and to make changes. The Dark moon when the moon is not visible for two to three days at a time is a time for letting go of all that is unessential to your life, for recognising accomplishments and planning for the future. Each month of the year the moon has a different name, the month of June being called a 'mead moon' or 'moon of horses'. In many ways the cycle of the moon has developed into a pre ordained set of rules which could be said to be fate. The phases and characteristics setting a preordained path and *we must restrain our desires in order to get by in a world whose order is pregiven.*[8]Some astrologers or prophets would believe that human behaviour changes depending on the type of the moon, the full moon for example often bringing out the more eccentric and strange facets of some people and increasing sexuality.

12th June 1858

My nerves are on edge as I anticipate Lily's arrival. I pace from one end of the room to the other, whilst trying to avoid polite conversation. The glass of whiskey I had ten minutes previous did nothing to calm my nerves.

I notice her immediately as she enters the room. The blue velvet dress suits her perfectly and accentuates the colour in her eyes. The red hair highlighted by the blue and shimmering in the light of the many candles. I excuse myself from the company and walk over to greet Lily. Taking her gloved hand in mine I raise it to my lips and kiss it while looking into her eyes. I notice that my actions bring a flush to her cheeks and she shyly looks away.

'Good evening. How has your day been in the company of the other women?'

'Virgil it has been one of the longest days of my life. They talk of nothing but cross stitch and the latest string quartets. I should much rather listen to a Beethoven symphony at least then there may be some musical surprises. I nearly interrupted their discussion of *Northanger Abbey* with some pearls of wisdom from the Marquis de Sade. I bit my tongue just in time. He may have been a great moralist but I doubt that the ladies would have appreciated what he has to teach'.

'That was perhaps wise. However, I should have liked to have seen their faces if you had started to tell them they needed disciplined. That would have been worth a pretty penny.

Would you like a glass of wine?'

'Yes a glass of burgundy would be nice'.

I pour a glass from the decanter on the table and reach it to Lily while escorting her to a seat in a quiet corner of the room.

'It is strange that these people who are so well educated cannot reach their own conclusions on anything. They give opinions on politics, culture and the weather and do not even think that what they are repeating may not be true. Tomorrow shall be a great day the sun shall be splitting the stones, yet, the cows rest under the trees and the sky is as red as sin. It will indeed be a good day for ducks or fishing'.

'Lily not everyone thinks as you do, not everyone has spent as much time in their own company questioning everything about the world. They are because of the nature of this world all sheep. They follow the wolf that will bring them the most power, wealth or standing in society. They do not question they follow. It is rare to find someone with their own thoughts about anything who is unashamed to voice their opinions for fear of ridicule'.

'I fear that I question too much. I fear that I question not enough. How else should I defeat my enemies if I do not think outside of our box? There must be more than idle conversation and hope. *If I wish to take advantage of the enemy I must perceive not just the advantage in doing so, I must first consider the ways he can harm me if I do*[9]. If I take advantage of my enemy would the conclusion be any different than if I didn't? Would the possibility of success outweigh the possibility of failure? I try to balance the scales and I am unsure of the justice on either side. If I know how to win, if I figure out how to live, maybe I may not necessarily succeed'.

'Have you had too much time to think while you were supposed to be distracting yourself with the company of others?'

---

[9] Sun Tzu, *The Art of War*

'I was surrounded by the other women yet it was as if we were oil and water and we would never mix. Yet I did not give myself away I did not settle. The dragons are the same but there is so much water that the oil on the surface should never be noticed. I must use that to my advantage. I am not yet sure how but I am certain I am closer to retribution if not a solution'.

I smile as I watch her, she is not as quiet as usual and is starting to trust me more...... I hope. Why else would she be as content to tell me all about her day and what she has been thinking?

She stops talking just long enough to take a breath.

'I think that I should retire for the evening I have quite exhausted myself with all this thinking and I must rise early tomorrow'.

I find myself asking her to stay a while longer. I was so enjoying the conversation, watching and listening. I do not want it to end.

She agrees as if she didn't really want to leave.

I move closer and take the hand resting on her knee in mine. It is soft and I find my fingers tracing the lines on her palm while she watches and I feel her hand slightly tremble.

'Do you like what you feel?' she asks, 'you are tracing those lines as if you are internalising every one'.

Perhaps I am storing them in my memory for when she is gone.

Then looking up at me she looks me in the eyes. Not from under timid eyelids this time, her gaze unwavering. 'I do not need a teacher, for I have not much to learn. I want you to master me. Know my thoughts, understand what I want without words, visualise my mind, know my soul, only then, will you master my body'

I cannot believe she wants me!

'I am the teacher who can give you exactly what it is you want and need, rewarding you with pleasure, rewarding you with pain, and I know you would want the same for me, you need shown who is in charge, and you think you can beat authority, but this authority has the ability to put you in your place, that place is under me......on top of me.....beside me, in any position we find ourselves in.......but you are my master.....ask and you shall receive.....your every desire is my command'.

Despite the fact there is a room full of people I take her hand and drawing Lily to her feet I lead her through the crowd to the closest stairs. Lifting the nearest candle without a word we climb slowly, the candlelight flickering on the darkened stairway. I watch her movements as she climbs one step in front of me. My heart beating so loudly in my chest I can hear it. She leads the way and as she opens the bedroom door I follow her over the threshold into the darkened room. Hands trembling I try to set the candle down on the bedside table only to send it crashing to the floor and throwing the room into shadows cast by the moon through the open curtains.

I can see her standing there in the darkness and make my way to her. Unable to contain my passions any longer I take her face in my hands and kiss her. She responds her mouth opening to let my tongue dance with hers. Deep kisses, long, her hands covering mine. I move one hand to her back drawing her closer to me the soft velvet crushed beneath my fingers and the other drawing her mouth to mine clasping her hair in my fist. I hear her moan softly and mimic my actions as she places her hand on my buttock pulling me closer, our bodies touching, my hardness fighting with the trousers for release. I don't want to rush, I want to savour every moment. Slowly I withdraw from her and stepping back I look at her as best I can in the shadowlight. I turn her around and run my hand up the hem of her dress touching the stockings at her ankles. I stroke her stocking covered legs while slowly inching her dress further up towards her waist. My hands touch the flesh at the top of her garters immediately sending surges of heat to my groin. I instruct her to bend over and place her hands on the bed.

She obeys.

I throw the skirt of the dress over her back and feel her buttocks, there are no under garments to cause any restrictions.

'Will you do as I ask?'

'Yes….anything', she replies.

Feeling the softness of her skin under my rough hands I pull back and gently smack her cheeks. She makes no sound. Then I repeat only a little harder, again no sound…..the third time I am sure I caused pain…..but she moans quietly with pleasure.

My hands pull her buttocks slightly apart and my fingers trace their way towards the top of her legs. My fingers feel the heat and the dampness between her legs. I rub gently and again hear her moan.

I've never wanted anything as much as I want to be inside her right now.

Pulling her skirt down I ask her to stand up. I take her hair placing it over her shoulder as I find the lace in the stays of her dress. I undo the laces and hooks pulling them apart and sliding her dress off her shoulders……letting it fall to the floor. My hands trace the line of her shoulders, the curve of her arms, and the swelling of her breasts. I take them in my hands gently squeezing her nipples as I kiss her neck and the lobe of her ear. Her hands cover mine, inviting me to hold her, showing me how she wants to be touched. Pushing her buttocks back against me she rubs against my hardness, teasing.

Then she moves one hand behind feeling for me placing her hand on my cock holding it, then gently rubbing through the material.

'It is not as I imagined it should feel….I had not realised that despite the flesh that it would feel so ….hard and yet smooth…..I want to feel all of you', she whispers.

Turning around she removes my dinner jacket throwing it to the floor. Then slowly she unbuttons my shirt then before sending it to join the jacket she runs her hands down my chest, gently squeezing each of my nipples on the way down. Her hands tracing the line from my belly button to the waistband of my trousers.

Gently she unhooks the fastenings and slides her hand inside. Her hands are cold to the touch and it momentarily calms the fire.

She slides my trousers to the floor and removes my boots.

I lie back on the bed and she joins me.

I feel the touch of our naked bodies and I pull her closer wanting to feel every inch of her silk like complexion. I bend her leg over mine as I kiss her cupping her buttock in my hand. Pulling her towards me …….I am very close to entering her ……but this is not about me. It's her first time and I want her to remember it …….and I want to remember forever.

Kissing her neck, her breasts, her stomach I kiss the mound at the top of her legs…….I push them apart so that she lies on the bed displayed in front of me. I rub her clit gently with the tip of my fingers and then my tongue. Slowly at first then quicker while my fingers probing at the entrance to her womb. She holds my head with her hands breathing heavily I can feel her trembling beneath me……her muscles tensing as she releases herself beneath me.

Then slowly I rise on top of her and with one swift stroke I am inside her.

I can feel her intake of breath.

'Did I hurt you?' I ask.

'Only for an instant …..please don't stop'.

I can barely contain myself I have waited so long for this and she is everything I ever wanted. I feel her muscles clenched tight around me and pull her closer to me my hands cupping her buttocks.

It is too much……..

I feel myself quicken my strokes …..

Then I feel myself release my seed inside her.

My arms trembling, I lie on her not wanting to move.

I can still feel her muscles spasm around my now limp cock.

'I am sorry I did not last longer….I wanted it to be everything you imagined and more but I just could not contain myself'.

'Virgil do not apologise. I have never wanted anything as much as I wanted to be with you I just wanted to feel you, to know what it was like to feel your touch. I had imagined it, but it was better than I imagined. I dreamt of how it would be to feel you inside me and know that in that moment that you were mine and I was yours'.

Feeling a slight chill in the air I pull the bed clothes out from beneath us and over our naked bodies.

I come back to earth with a sudden jolt.

No one can ever even suspect that I have been with Lily. They can never know that she is no longer pure. They cannot know that she is mine and I am hers. It must be our secret no matter how much we may wish to tell the world. I have been such a fool both of us have thrown caution to the wind and anyone could have seen us leave the dining room. Anyone could have watched or followed. Despite the fact that I want to do nothing more than stay in her arms, in this bed. I must move, I must go back downstairs and act as if nothing has happened.

She will be feel that I have used her now if I leave, but what choice do I have.

Gently I pull the hair from across her face and tuck it behind her ear. I kiss her softly on the neck and whisper, 'I must leave you for a while. We had forgotten that others may have been watching us. I must go back downstairs and keep up appearances. I am sorry. I want nothing more than to be able to stay here but we must be careful'.

I can feel the atmosphere rather than see her reaction. Despite the coolness she replies with, 'You are right of course, please do not be long'.

She squeezes my hand as I release her and wraps herself in the rest of the bed clothes as I get out from under them. The candlelight has gone and I do my best with the light of the moon to find my clothes and put them back on in some semblance of order.

I fear that I shall be wearing more than my clothes as I tentatively walk down the stairs keeping to the shadows. I fear my face wears a mask of everything I have just done and that everyone who looks at me should know.

I breathe deeply as I walk down the corridor towards the noise and the smell of stale tobacco and alcohol. Thankfully the door is open and I can see the setup of the room before I enter. I slip back into the reveries as if nothing just happened and pouring myself a drink join in the with the now not so polite conversation.

I sit there in a daze. My mind is there half listening and feigning interest...the other half blocking out the buzz of noise as I relive the moments upstairs. It is some hours before I notice that most of the guests have left and that there are just a handful of gentlemen in various stages of stupefaction dotted at intervals around the room. I wait until the final carriage has left before I can relax a little and return to bed.

I am sure that Lily is probably sound asleep by now so I do not disturb her and go to my own room.

13th June 1858

I did not sleep much, when I eventually came to bed. I do believe I saw the dawn approaching when eventually the final beat of the horses hooves had faded in the distance. I could not help but replay over and over everything which had occurred with Lily on the previous evening. It was as if time had stood still but I am sure we had not been together very long. In my panic I had envisaged us having been away from the crowd for hours when in essence it could not have been one.

Yet it seemed longer.

I had lain under the linen sheets arms about the covers cool in the morning air, but I did not seem to notice. Now I am awake looking at the folded sashes of the bed curtains hanging in swags around my head. Not something I am fond of......too many frills and dust..... so much dust. Why would anyone want to hang material over their head? I can understand that in aristocratic homes perhaps it is essential to hide away from the servants when still asleep but I prefer to be able to breathe rather than be stifled by the unessential tradition. Who after all is going to be interested in my nocturnal behaviour?

Who indeed?

Again I replay the sight of Lily in my head or what I imagined she had looked like in the darkness. Words of one of Coleridge's poems pop into my head *Twas partly love and partly fear, and partly twas a bashful art, that I might rather feel than see, the swelling of her heart.* Love, now there's something I've been afraid to feel, fear seems normal these days.

I am sure she would not be happy this morning, but I hoped she understood that it was a necessity to abandon her as I did.

I know I will not sleep now and it must be time for breakfast. Casting aside last night's clothes the stench of stale tobacco hanging on every fibre. I could not bear to wear them. I check the closet for a clean linen shirt and trousers and once dressed head into the landing. Outside Lily's room I put my ear to the door and listen for movement. I hear nothing and knock gently on the door. Pushing it ajar on squeaky hinges I look inside, the room is empty. I am overcome with guilt. Perhaps it would have been easier to face her in the confines of her room as over the dining table surrounded by the ears of others.

In a repeat of last night I tentatively descend the stairs, again with the feeling that I am about to face a hanging squad. This time though I cannot hide in the shadows for the sunlight is already shining through the sashes and dancing off the silver onto the red velvet walls. I take a deep breath and steady my pulse before pushing open the dining room door. The smell of breakfast greets me and despite the fact I am dreading having to talk to Lily about last night, she isn't there. I check the drawing room and library without avail.

She definitely isn't in the house.

Returning to the dining room I eat in a per functionary manner unable to taste anything and in a daze. I hear myself chewing and the sounds of the Westminster clock ticking away the seconds.....a continuous tick tock tick tock.....it's as if it is telling me to beware of the time. Whiling away the seconds afraid to talk, afraid to actually think about what is really annoying me. Afraid that there isn't enough time that there really isn't any hope. How much time do we have left? Days......eight days. Eight days until they take her from me, until they close our box, until they take away hope.

I finish what is on the plate and go in search of my walking boots and overcoat. Despite the sun it is still early and morning air will be damp and cool.
She cannot be too far away......I hope.

I walk through the bottom garden and notice the footprints in the dew covered moss. She has at least come in this direction. Climbing the style I stand on top of it to see if I can make out any shape or movements on the horizon.

Nothing but cows.

We had only been in two directions since arriving and I do not think that she would have headed to the town on her own. I therefore head in the direction of the old house and the graveyard.

I head up the hill almost blinded by the early morning sun and almost tripping over the odd hardened cow pat. The ground undulates where the cows had trodden the ground when it has been wet. When I reach the top of the hill I can just about make out the view of the valley. I spot her sitting on a stone wall a couple of fields away; At least I presume it is her in that revolting coloured overcoat.

A new briskness about my step I head in her direction playing over in my head what I am going to say.

Lily hears me approaching from behind her and turns her head in my direction; she does not rise from her seat. I climb over the wall and sit down beside her. I do not know what to say, it is unlike me to be lost for words. I could say what she wants to hear; I could make something up and spin a version of events which would be political to getting me out of bother. I find for the first time I have nothing to say, I do not know what to say as I know I should have stayed with her but .....I could not. We sit in silence for some minutes before she speaks.

'You know I do not blame you for leaving me last night. You were right in doing so it would not be a good thing if you were to be found with me. I would not want to be responsible for getting you in trouble. However, if things had been different I would have enjoyed lying with you a while longer, waking up beside you and discovering more ways to please you. I have never wanted anything as much as I wanted you last night. It is just a shame circumstances are against us'.

'I feel awful I didn't just want to have sex with you and get up and leave like I may have done with some common whore. I wanted to enjoy the moment also but I think the feelings of lust got the better of me. I could blame it on alcohol but I had very little and to do so would be to diminish what happened. I do not want you to think I just wanted your body, when in truth every word we have spoken these last few weeks has been foreplay; I got as much pleasure from your words and thoughts as from touching you. I loved everything about it. The question is what do we do now? Can we continue as we are over the next few weeks and pretend to others nothing has happened and that you are still my slave. We should really run away somewhere they would never find us, but is there anywhere like that?'

I get off the cold stones and pull Lily to her feet. I have a sudden urge to go visit the waterfall. Taking her by the hand I lead over the fields until we get near the church. I had forgotten it was Sunday. Taking the back entrance passed the farm as we had done previously, we arrive at the group of trees, and a circular area of land that some may call a fairy copse. To the top end of the trees is a mill surrounded by ancient stone walls. No one is about today. The mill wheel feeds the water to the mill unaware it can have the day off...and then the water of the river flows down over the stones and disappears into the trees.

Walking around the edge of the stone wall we climb down the bank which is partially covered in nettles and weeds. It is slippy in the morning dew. Following the wall we turn the bend and go straight down to the river. I take Lily's hand and guide her down the last of the steep bank to the stones at the river's edge. Looking to our left we can see the waterfall splashing into the pool beneath in a white frothy mass.

'Saint Patrick was supposed to have baptised the people that lived in the hamlet at the top of the hill in these waters. The hamlet long since gone, the area is mostly surrounded by farmers now. The cave there', I point to the other side of the river bank, 'was supposed to have been the last resting place of one of Robert the Bruce's knights. It is rumoured that he was buried with all his possessions and gold. Although I do not think they could actually have got a body in the cave I do think he is perhaps buried nearby.

Sometimes when I was young I used to lie in bed at night and imagine finding the treasure and what I would like to do with it when I found it; All that gold and jewellery, his sword and armour....I would remove the sword from his bony grip, put on the metal clothes and walk down the main street of the town and buy a horse and a lot of sweets. On other occasions I could afford to buy my parents a new house or a field, something that would enable them to keep themselves when they were older. I suppose it did not occur to me then that something like that could be worth a good deal more than horses and sweets'.

'But do you think he was actually buried here? It is probably just rumour but some of them are based in a certain amount of fact. I suppose the fact that they fought a few fields from here may have added to the myth'.

'Other men and women have been working in the mill on many an evening when they have reported to have seen an old woman in black rags sitting on the top of the older derelict building at the top of the waterfall and the sound of her screaming could be heard above the crashing of the mill wheel and the rumble of the machinery. Although it is said that the crashing of water down the rocks and into the pool can resemble the sound of wailing and combined with that and the wind in the trees, I am sure there have been many a frightened worker.

I used to love coming down here in the evenings along with many of the other village boys and swimming in the cold water.'

Looking at the water now I can tell it is freezing cold despite the month. The water just has that look about it; dark and very green with mossy slime. It's like looking at a cup of tea and before tasting it you know it's going to be cold despite the steam.

'There used to be a lot of frogspawn about here in the pools inside the cave. I used to come down with a jar and fill it up and take the green slime home to hatch into frogs. Mother never liked to see me bringing that; she didn't like the frogs jumping about the yard'.

'Would you like to look in the cave?'

Looking at her feet I realise her black lace boots would not be suitable to cross the rocky path across the middle of the river.

'Perhaps you should take your boots off; the rocks are smooth enough that you will not cut your feet'.

She bends to remove her boots one hand steadying herself on my shoulder. There isn't very much room between the edge of the river and the edge of the stone wall. I forget she would also be wearing stockings. She pulls her skirts up to remove them giving me more than a glimpse of the garter tops and the smallest glimpse of flesh on her thigh. No other under garments. The sight is enough to change my perfectly innocent thoughts into something a lot more. I watch as she slides each stocking slowly down over the white skin of her thighs, her calves and her feet. The movement of the silk against the skin has me captivated, despite the fact that there is a very naked mound of flesh at the top of her legs. Uncovered..... Inviting...... The second stocking is removed and placed inside her boots. I decide to lead the way onto the first rock, it is slippy. I then move to the second rock so that I can reach out a hand to Lily and guide her to the first. I reach across and in an instant I have slipped on the wet moss and landed with a splash in the river. The whole thing happens in a matter of seconds before I even have a chance to steady myself.

The river isn't deep at this section but is not shallow and I find I am soaked entirely.

I'm winded and embarrassed.......and I was right...... the water is cold!

Lily takes one look at me and starts to laugh.........maybe I'll see the funny side later.

I stand up and wade back to the bank. Shivering already I decide to remove my clothes and at least wring out some of the water. The linen material is heavy with the weight. I remove my coat and boots, then peel the shirt off me, it wants to stay glued to my skin with the water. Lastly I remove my trousers with difficulty trying very hard not to lose balance and land in the nettles.

Lily watches I can almost read her thoughts from the look in her eyes. Despite the fact I am shivering all over I find that I am aroused by her watching. She blushes slightly as she becomes aware that I have read her thoughts.

Despite the fact the water was colder than the arctic I suggest she joins me for a swim. I think we should be safe enough and while everyone is at church we should have no audience.

Slowly she unbuttons the ridiculous dress and coat revealing her corset and nothing else beneath. I gently turn her around and undo the laces at the back loosening the material around her breasts. I pull the corset over her head then casting it aside, hold her hands above her head with one hand while I pull her hair to the side and kiss the back of her neck slowly. I can feel the goosebumps appear on her arms and hope that I have caused them and not the cold. Letting go of her arms I move my hands around to cup her breasts, gently tugging on her erect nipples. She moves back against me rubbing her cheeks against my now throbbing cock, her hands behind her feeling my thighs.

I move away and watch her turn around. She looks so much different in the light, but still as pale. Her skin is almost translucent and slightly blue. Moving to the waters edge I kneel down at the deeper side just under the waterfall and jump in. She hesitates.

'It's not all that cold, I lie, between chattering teeth'. I splash her with the water and she knows I am lying. She doesn't dip her toe in the edge but just takes one jump and l catch her as she lands.

'This water isn't cold Virgil we will both catch pneumonia, maybe that would be a blessing'.

Grabbing her around the middle I kiss her softly at first, but I cannot get enough of her. My tongue enters her mouth touching hers. My hands do not know what they are at I do not know what part of her I want to touch first. Her hands gently cup my face, tentative and unsure while I'm trying to devour her. It's as if she is unsure what she should do or what I would want her to do.

Removing her hands I kiss her neck, moving downwards to her breasts cupping them as I suck on her nipples, biting gently I can hear her gasp with the new sensations, her hands now on the top of my head. I do not move further down although I would have liked to but I fear I may have drowned. Again kissing her lips I feel her hand on my cock rubbing gently across the tip and slowly pulling my skin downwards. She pulls away from me and moves so that she can watch what effect her movements are having on me, watching, fascinated with her new found toy. My hand finds the top of her legs pushing them slightly part as I move my fingers between them. Gently touching her lips, it is hard to tell if she is very aroused or the water is deceptive, my fingers finding their way inside her as she continues to pleasure me. I can't take it any longer I pull her towards me and placing my hands under her buttocks I lift her up over my cock, the water helping to support her weight.

'Guide me in' I beg.

One hand between us she guides my cock inside her. Slowly to start she is still very tight. She moves a little further down my shaft with every stroke until I am filling her entirely. A fast learner her pussy clamping my cock as if she would not let go sucking me in with her clenching muscles. Slowly at first, with deep strokes bobbing up and down in the water, she lets go of me the water supporting her as she lies back floating on the top of the water her legs gripping my waist for dear life. She watches as I fuck her, my cock moving quickly now I do not want to release first but I fear that is going to happen. She looks me straight in the eyes no need for words. I feel as if I am possessed by the devil himself. My muscles tense and between clenched teeth I cannot hold any longer and I let out a low growl as I cum inside her. She does not say a word but just smiles teasing me as she knows what effect she is having on my senses. Pulling her back up her arms again around my neck I kiss her again. Soft kisses, not as urgent. Although I do feel if I wasn't now shivering under weakened legs I would start all over again.

The Eight of Swords

The final card in the tarot series is a desolate image of the maiden in the eight of swords; it paints a picture of isolation, restriction and despair. The prominent image of the woman, who is bound, blindfolded and surrounded by a metal prison of swords. She stands alone on marshy ground, the dismal grey skies showing a lack of hope and in the distance can be seen a town. The woman has been separated from what she knows and the familiarity that brings protection.

She is restricted by the circumstances that she currently finds herself in with very few options yet she is blind to her freedom as the blindfold prevents her seeing the clear path beneath her feet.

Confusion is caused as there is uncertainty in which way to turn or which path to take, an overwhelming feeling of loss leaving her powerless and awaiting rescue. Yet the blindfold itself is a metaphor for physiological entrapment. She has blinkered herself to other avenues of escape as she lacks the freedom and choice to make decisions. The representation of someone backed into a corner that needs to stop and re-evaluate their options. They need to think rationally how they may overcome the difficulties they face, the enforced isolation and lack of freedom. They may be blindfold and bound but the feet are not tied. This card shows there is always a way out of any given situation. It is important to try and reassess options and overcome fear. Grey skies do eventually blow over and wet ground dries up. It is important not to fear the unknown.

The Eight of Swords can also indicate that the person will meet the love of their life. The one person they will forever love completely with an all consuming passion. Combined with the Devil card the isolation and feeling of imprisonment can be compounded, while the moon may also lead our feelings astray. It is therefore essential with this tarot card to contemplate an exit from imprisonment by every and any possible means.

I look in the gilded oval shaped chevaille the signs of age as vivid as my own, the once smooth surface blackened with age and the light refracting in odd direction, the bevelled edges as black as soot. It is at times as if I am in a fairground attraction and my likeness being changed in a hall of mirrors for my own amusement.

When you look in the mirror, what do you see?

I suppose to every person and location it varies. It depends on perspective or frame of mind. The picture you see is not just a reflection of a person, people or things; it's a time, a place, a thought, a feeling and in essence a reflection of all these things. What we see externally is a projection of what is being processed internally. Often it is said that if we could see people's souls, we may see them differently, in a different perspective or light. When we look in a mirror, in some shape or form we see our own soul. If you are looking in a mirror to catch a glimpse of what is happening behind you in a room, to secretively watch the movement of others, perhaps to check your appearance, whether your hat is straight or your tie is slanted, to view what you look like at the end of the day......or the start.

Perhaps it is vanity that you use it for, perhaps it is stealth, or just to see what the world looks like from a different perspective. If you were to ask everyone in a room to stand in the one spot they would all see something different, something that only their soul can see or feel.

Often as I look in this mirror I see her reflection, a mirage...or imagine that I see just the smallest glimmer of her reclined on the red velvet chaise in the drawing room, her skin the colour of fine French porcelain and almost as transparent. The memory frequently ruminates in my mind.

Lily had woken that morning and joined me at the dining table. I sat reading 'The Northern Whig', silently, as her cutlery clinked on the stoneware plate. I remember thinking that the noise was irritating, but despite this I was enjoying the silent companionship.

'How will you remember me?' she asked, 'in ten years time, how will you remember......what I look like?'

'I have all I need here in my mind, my memories, although there are not many, there are enough. I can see and feel everything we have witnessed and encountered'.

'Surely how you see me shall diminish like the holding capacity of glue. My image will be there for a while then it will fade around the edges before it eventually disappears'.

Putting down the paper I stand up and walk around the table. I sit on the edge. Taking her face in my hands I hold it and look into those large blue eyes.

'Nothing will let me forget your face. Nothing!

My eyes pass over each contour of her face, as she blushes and bites her bottom lip; a brief smile twinkles in her eyes. Just briefly, before a shutter is replaced and her sad eyes turn downwards, eyelids almost closed as they face the floor.

'I wish we had met sooner and in different circumstances. I should like to have known all of you. Not just the man who is taking each day at a time, worrying about me....you do worry....I can see it in your eyes'.

Lily lifts her eyes up to look into mine.

'I should like to know the man who can relax when he comes home for the evening, what you do to pass the time, who you talk to, the silly everyday thoughts, what your favourite colour is, your most prized memory, your worst fear, how you react when you lie, although I think I should be able to read your face like a book even after the first time we talked. If I knew you were lying I do not think I would say. I am sure you would have your reasons.

I would like to know what it feels like to lie with you at night and for you to be the first thing I see in the morning. These last few days I woke up and all I could think of was you....I'd look over and see the empty bed and realise that some things are nothing but dreams. You've given me a new reason to live........but you also have the power to take that away. It feels like I've been waiting for you, waiting for a light to shine in the dark.

I guess I just want to know that someone will remember me when I am gone. I hate to think that I shall just disappear, that no one will remember my name and in the blink of an eye I shall be gone as if I never existed. Perhaps it is vanity, but I want to believe I meant something to someone'.

Lily gives the impression that she is strong.....but her eyes tell a different story. She is fighting a lot of demons.

'We have now, we cannot wish anything else although believe me I do wish more. Honestly I cannot remember the last time I relaxed at home. It was probably before my son died, he was the reason I came home from work. Evenings then were not as long they passed without me even realising weeks were not past.

My favourite colour, I am not sure, I like to paint a lot with blues and reds, although in these last few years it has been the darker hues. I used to just empty my mind onto the canvas and my worries were gone. Now I see what I paint and that worries me more. I suppose in a way it is like a diary of my feelings, only instead of painting words with ink, I paint shapes with oil.

I have never really talked or spent time with very many people.......at least not since moving to Belfast. I used to talk a lot more and go out on walks with my wife and child. These days I hide away with my bottle of whisky and a book.

My most cherished memory to date was the birth of my son. I did not really love my wife but in time I grew fond of her, maybe I did love her in my own way. Those were happier days.

My worst fear used to be that I would let my parents down, that I would not live up to their expectations. I did let them down and in the end I left and didn't go back. Then I feared for the life of my son and what should become of him because of 'The Order'. God saw fit to relieve me of both of these fears. I've not really been afraid of losing my own life for some time, for years I have been numb to death. I suppose with what I have seen death is a way of life.

Now, I fear for you and that I cannot do anything to change your future. Yes I worry. If God even exists his blueprint for life is truly flawed and I suppose those with artistic abilities feel things so much more when they are alone with so many thoughts. God will let them take you from me and I now fear a future without you in it. I've never felt anything quite like it, and the memory of your face is only the beginning.

I don't suppose there is anyone in the town that is able to take a chrystollium of you......of us. If I can find some paint and a canvas....I am sure there is some in the house. The upper class always like to think they are artists and connoisseurs. I will paint your picture myself and I will get to look at you for a few hours without having to find an excuse'.

Kissing her on the forehead I don't wait for a reply. I leave the room to look for the paints. It turned out to be not as hard a task as I presumed. Pulling out the dresser drawers in the drawing room I find a large cache. Finding a blank canvas proves a little harder. There are however, plenty of horrible paintings on the walls, choosing one by someone I do not recognise, I find some white paint and cover over the top of the dreadful tulips and wait a few hours for it to dry.

Finding Lily we discuss how and where she would like to be painted and remembered. Surprisingly she chooses to be painted in the four poster bed draped in folds of material. Apparently it's a bit like the French style before the revolution.

'When you look at your work, you will hopefully think of more than my face' she said smiling.

We arrange the linens and furniture and find some other materials, of course the obligatory red velvet that seems to be hanging around the whole house.

Lily removes her clothes and drapes herself in the material so it protects her modesty, one leg hanging provocatively over the edge of the bed. She moves and the loose material exposes one of her very edible looking nipples. Fighting the desire to join Lily on the bed I get all my materials and palette in order and begin.

Firstly I do a rough sketch of the setting on the canvas, making sure I have all the proportions and shapes correct.

'This is just how I would imagine Rubens, Titian or Boticelli working with their muses, painting their visions. Sometimes I wonder what it would have been like to live then, in Renaissance Europe. Everything seemed to have been so much more enlightened, bolder, colourful and free.

Lily talks while I continue to paint.

'I would have fitted in well with my red hair, perhaps in a past life I would have modelled for the masters. I am sure society would have frowned upon it, but, I do not think I would have cared. It would be lovely to have the freedom to do what pleases yourself and to not be judged. To have the ability to create what you envisage is certainly a gift'.

Her skin is almost as pale as the white paint already on the canvas. A very little Naples yellow is needed just to add a little contrast. I start with the lightest paints and then the largest blocks of darker red and black. The sunlight shining through the sash windows means she is partially bathed in light and a shadow cast over her face. Ironically the shadows do not seem to drown the luminescent features. It is a little like her personality, she doesn't let the shadows cast by the dark clouds affect everything else that is going on.

1883

Thinking of that day always makes me smile and when I look at the painting I do think, and feel, more than I can see.

When I had finished painting she was so excited to see the finished product, she perched herself on the edge of the bed on her knees, naked. I turned the painting to face her; she remained silent as she studied it. She looked so lost as the single tear fell on her cheek, no more.....just one, before she wiped it away.

'I could have fitted in quite well', was all she said.

I had placed the painting back on the easel and sat on the edge of the bed. When I see her face that is how I see her now. Naked, vulnerable, sitting between the bedposts, her eyes wide and face flushed. Holding her two hands in her lap, fidgeting scared to show what she is really thinking and feeling. Looking in her eyes I took her face in my hands and kissed her, pulling her towards me. We were both drowning and I could not breathe. Slowly we lay down, slowly fingers brushed flesh, at least it felt that way. Almost as if time stood still, feeling, touching, caressing, every part of her engrained on my memory. Closing my eyes now I can relive every second......and feel it! While more than a single tear escapes.

Most people these days buy art to be seen to be displaying their wealth. The only painting I now possess holds a lifetime of memories. Every picture tells a story, if only they could talk......what a story she would tell.

15th June 1858

Whirring and turning, whirring and turning, faster and faster the tin colours blur into each other, no longer a discernible shape or picture but a whirlpool of colours, a kaleidoscope without a purpose. Ever since I unwrapped the carefully folded brown paper package and removed the string, it started, spinning out of control and without aid.

The spinning top moved on its own accord, whirring and turning, whirring and turning. I watched from above through the fog as if through someone else's eyes. Then the mist takes over and through the dim light I can see a large wooden mill wheel turning on its own accord. I can hear the splash and rumble as it turns in the water. It turns and a body emerges from the water, limp, entirely immersed in water on every turn of the wheel; baptised repeatedly in the name of the Lord.

Suddenly, the eyes of the woman open and in the blink of an eye she is no longer captive but floating against the current towards me as if she is walking on water. She is almost in front of me, or above, I cannot tell which. Her face is marked, pitted, diseased, decayed. The blue eyes out of place in such a face look straight through me. Her hand outstretched, reaching, begging as the noise of distant bells sound, vibrating, ringing, a warning chime. Hands still outstretched an invisible force pulls her backwards into the fog, and in an instant she is gone. A single chime echoes in the darkness.

I gradually regain consciousness and realise I can hear the grandfather clock in the hall striking the last of its Westminster chimes. The mist has cleared and brought me back to reality once more and a rather bleak feeling in the pit of my stomach.

I feel empty.
Unnerved.

The dream felt so real. Like I was there......... Watching.

The onlooker at an execution.

The 'witch' drowned at the wheel just to see if she could save herself. A woman killed because others are too afraid of what they do not understand, destroyed by the disease of prejudice held in men's hearts.

It is a while since I have thought of God's wrath. Only a cruel God would let others die in his name, without proof or reason.

How can someone so omnipotent and who 'raises people from the dead' let others die in his name? The more I see of this world, I do not believe in his existence, yet I want to.........

I want to hope that somehow he would help those who believe.

Rising from my bed I dress and break my fast quickly. On the way through the hall I grab a long coat and hat from the hall stand and leave the house. I head over the fields to the church.

Pushing open the heavy oak door, I am immediately greeted by the humid smell of damp and dust, typical of the old stone buildings with no fires or much air circulation.

Leaving the door ajar behind me I enter the sparse hallway and walk across the stone floor. There are two doors to either side of me; I have a choice of entrances. The first door on either side would take me to either the left or right balcony overlooking the pulpit. The second set of doors to either side of the main body of the church on the ground floor.

I move to the second right hand door and pull it towards me using the large brass handle. Crossing the threshold I inhale deeply taking in the old familiarity of the building.

I feel slightly uneasy as if I am trespassing on someone's private property.

The pews at the back are in single file, for those of us who have less money to place in the offering plate. Those closest to the pulpit have family pews each with their own door. Moving down the rows I find the McAuley tag. There is nothing like the hypocrisy of 'keeping up appearances' even if the pew was more often empty than full.

I pull it towards me and sit myself on the blue velvet pew cushion.

I remember sitting on the back pews in winter, the hard wooden boards so cold my backside hurt. There were no fancy comforts for me in those days.

I sit for a short while taking in the surroundings. I read the names on the stained glass windows, in memory of people who can afford not to be forgotten. One depicts farmers and the harvest and another is dedicated to those lost in war. Stained glass is so very creative, and so expensive. I spent many a Sunday morning staring at the patterns the colours were making on the floor or ceiling. It used to help pass the time while the minister preached his sermon to the God fearing flock.

My eyes look to the steps spiralling around the pulpit. Barley twisted oak wood adorned with the inset of a burning bush and the words 'Ardens sed Virens', burning but flourishing, dead but alive, an illusion.

The only change in my current surroundings is the vantage point from which I can take in the details. Everything has remained unchanged in the passing years.

Why am I here?

I suppose my dream reminded me of the colours in the windows dancing around in the light, controlled only by the sun and passing clouds. Partially I am reminded that my mother would always say, 'God will always provide what we need'. She would say I needed to have faith.

In turn this makes me think of God asking Abraham to sacrifice Isaac his only son; the son who he had waited well into his old age for his wife to conceive, the one thing which was most important to him. Abraham didn't give up his faith in God and was prepared to do as he asked. God of course provided him with an alternative sacrifice, a ram caught in a hedge. God provided what was needed or required at the last moment.

I can't help but compare Isaac to Lily. I am not Abraham, however, but one of twelve unwilling disciples. I find it hard to believe that an alternative sacrifice will be provided. God has nothing to do with the plans of The Dragons. I am sure whatever God they worship has a different perspective.

I blindly clutch at the hope that if I offer a prayer, everything will work out as it should. Fate and hope are not always two things which marry well. When someone's path or destiny is already foretold, the only way to change that is with huge upheaval or to wage war on 'the powers that be', whether that is a monarch or a dictator. These plans take years of plotting and vast numbers of people.

I cannot fight the fire of a dragon on my own; I would not even know how to begin to protect myself.

For years now I have hidden in the darkness and stayed out of the limelight. Everything seems different now. The picture is frayed around the edges, blurred beyond belief. I no longer know what is black and white as the colours bleed together in the canvas of my mind. I pray God will provide the answer to my dilemma.

Absent minded I pick up the dusty bible from the corner of the pew. It looks like it hasn't been opened in a very long time. Opening it at the first page I notice it contains the McAuley family tree, births, deaths and marriages, but it is incomplete. There are no entries after the birth of the current head of the household.

I bring the Bible with me as I leave the church. It is quite a heavy tome compared to the small everyday Bible my family shared. This is an ornate leather bound copy with brass fastenings and painted illustrated lettering, a really expensive work of art that has been made to last. For years the genealogy of the family could be recorded and marked for posterity.

I fully intend to add Emily and Lucas to their rightful places when I return to the house. I do not know whether my calligraphy writing would be good enough. Perhaps Lily could do it for me.

When I enter the house it is rather quiet. I find that Lily has gone for a walk to pick more herbs and wild foods. Obviously she has decided not to leave the cooking to the experts as she had mentioned. Cook informed me that Lily had wanted to try out a few other dishes with pigeon and duck.

'I hope Lily hasn't been disturbing you or giving you extra work? You don't look well. Cook is very pale with dark shadows below her eyes.

'I've had dreadful stomach cramps the last few days, sir, and I am very tired. I think I may be sickening for something......although I hope it will pass'.

'If you need anything just let me know. I'm not above making my own food for a day or two'.

Cook thanks me and ensuring me all will be well, I leave her to her baking.

After the evening meal I show Lily the Bible and ask if she could fill in the blanks in calligraphy writing.

Fetching a rather expensive looking fountain pen from the library I instruct Lily what to write:

Emily McAuley b.27th April 1829 – d.18th January 1847

Married

Virgil Black   b. 2? February 1827 –

Son: Lucas Black b. 5th September 1846 – d.18th January 1847

There is now at least some reference to their lives even if it is only in the family Bible. In some way it will also have to act as their tombstones.

I often hypothesise about how my life may have turned out, if I had not been a stupid child who could not keep his cock in his trousers. Would I be the landowner of the now dilapidated farm?

Running my own shop?

Would I be at home with my family, sitting around a large farmhouse table, surrounded by the aroma of home baked bread and the staple vegetable broth? I suppose I could be anywhere doing anything, given that the one mistake I did make has brought me to where I am now.

I look at the chaise in the drawing room, as I have done several times these last few days. Something still puzzles me.....how did they know I would make the mistake? I suppose it is human nature to give into our weaknesses. Is there ever a time when the result of our actions does not have a price?

I've been here in this room so many times now. I have watched the echo of my own memories played out before me, I am a spectator of my own folly.

Mr. McAuley said they had watched me.

I am consumed by more embarrassment now than I had been at the time. I suppose it is possible that panic consumed me in that moment; there was no room for other emotions.

They had watched me.......

I leave the drawing room and check for a sign of a door in the walls in the hall. There are no other entrances visible until the next room. I enter the next door which is the study; there are no other doors in this room just another fireplace back to back with the other.

There must be a secret passageway or door, a lever, an entrance in one of the other walls; otherwise they could not have viewed us as they stated.

I tap the walls and look for any sign of an entrance or keyhole.

Nothing is visible.

I pull the oil lamps at either side of the fireplace, remove the books from their shelves, push the furniture out of the way, I look under the awning of the unlit fire. Yet, I cannot find any possible entrance. Stepping back out of the hearth, my foot catches on the rug. I trip and fall backwards, winding myself for a few brief moments and bruising my pride.

I sit to catch my breath.

A draft flows up from a small letter box shaped vent underneath the black marble hearth. Putting my hand up to it I feel there is more of a breeze than I should have thought necessary in such a big room. On closer inspection the outer brass casing looks as if it is on hinges. I pull the top towards me. I hear grinding and a series of clicking sounds beneath me.

Then they stop.

Standing up I push the rest of the rug out of the way, the wooden polished floor does not look out of place.

There must be a door, I heard the mechanism.

Now that I have a space cleared I stand on the hearth and once again bend down to pull the lever.

Again I hear the clicking sounds.

This time, however, a rectangular shaped area pops up out of the floor.

A door, a hatch, a lid?

My weight must have kept it from opening the first time.

Unconsciously I take a rather large breath before pulling the hatch upwards.

Beneath me a set of stone steps disappears into the darkness.

I retrieve a candle stick and tapers from the desk and using the matches I light the tallow candle. I put the spill matches into my pocket. I don't want to get stuck in the dark. Cupping the frame with my hand to prevent the draft extinguishing it, I slowly descend into the unknown depths.

There does not appear to be a banister or sides to the stairway so I move slowly, one foot after the other. Thirteen steps in total and the closer to the bottom I get, the colder the air feels. It is not surprising due to the amount of stone surrounding me. On reaching the bottom I turn around slowly so as to take in my surroundings. To either side of the stone stairway there appears to be a passageway. On the wall to the left, which I would expect to be directly beneath the fireplace there is a metal ladder. On inspection I find that the ladder is attached to the wall by metal rivets. On the wall there are also a number of oil lamps at regular intervals. I light the closest using the candle and at once I am surrounded by a corridor of long flickering shadows.

Setting down my candlestick I shake the ladder firmly to check it is safe, before climbing. On reaching the top I find a small sliding panel. I push it across and at once I am blinded by daylight. I also have a direct view of the red chaise. The panel must come half way up the wall of the room.

Pushing back the panelling I descend the steps.

How could anyone be bothered climbing a ladder and waiting for an indefinite period just to trap another? Personally I wouldn't be troubled....but then I did not have an agenda.

Retrieving my candle I walk to the right hand side of the steps and start to follow the passageway, slowly lighting the wall lamps as I pass.
Despite the chill and dampness of the surroundings I find myself sweating profusely.

I probably should not be down here but I don't think there is anyone in the house except Lily and the sick cook.

I walk to the right hand side of the steps and find that they are placed in the middle of one corridor which is lined with doors. On closer inspection I realise they are cells. Each heavy wooden door with a small barred metal lattice opening. I slide across the stiff barred lock. Slowly I pull the door towards me. Everything smells damp of mildew and mice. Shining the candle around I can see it is a small room just big enough for a small bed. On each wall there are round metal hoops, similar to those found in a farmyard for tying up horses. I exit the cell and close the door. I notice the small channel drain running the length of the corridor floor.

Was it here that they brought Lily when they killed the other girls?

I open a few more doors to be greeted by almost identical views. In some the metal rings have handcuffs attached.

I know exactly what has happened here. I am reminded of the times I have spent with Donna in an almost similar environment. These rooms however lack the comfort of the cells I had been in before.

These cells look like they have not been used in some years. They also look a lot older than the house by a good few hundred years. The stone work is similar to that found in the castle walls in Templepatrick and Carrickfergus. There must be

159

over twenty rooms down this corridor and I hadn't even looked in the other direction yet.

I shiver as I think that these men have become a lot more open in their activities, passing their shenanigans off as drunken parties surrounded by prostitutes. It is after all the oldest trade in the world, but how old is the order?

I retrace my steps and walk towards the stone staircase, passing by the opposite side this time. I follow the corridor again lighting the oil lamps as I go. There are not as many doors in this corridor, but a lot of ladders. I walk to the end and find two solid oak doors. I push at them but they do not move. Both are locked and therefore I shall have to imagine the contents.

Setting my candle down I climb the last ladder and push across the small panel. When my eyes become accustomed to the light again I realise I am just behind the kitchen stove. I can hear movement and looking to my left I see cook at the table and Lily appearing to comfort her.

Lily heads in my direction and lifting the kettle from the stove fills a cup sitting on the sideboard.

'A cup of tea will do you good' Lily says.

Cook does not move. Lily then bends down to remove a tin from under the white Belfast sink. She opens it and puts two tea spoonfuls of the white powder in the tea.

That definitely wasn't sugar she put in cook's tea.

From my tremulous position on the ladder I cannot make out any words on the tin. White powder could be anything from bicarbonate of soda to rat poison.
Sweating now due to the heat of the stove I climb back to solid ground.

What is she up to?

Leaving the oil lamps lit I walk back to the stone stairway. I climb the steps quicker than I descended. I feel a chill in the air and I do not wish to spend any more time in the darkness. The secret prison has me feeling dirty.

On reaching the study I close the latch and replace the carpet before sitting at the Davenport desk to recover my composure. My head does not know what to make of all these secrets.

Who had been in the cellar the night Emily had been with me in the drawing room?

After all they were apparently held up by a cousin when I had arrived that evening.

Was it here they had held Lily?

Was she here the night I destroyed my life?

It is strange how we often cross paths with people but never meet them or notice them until fate intends.

I feel depressed. I do not know what to do, think or say. I do not like this form of darkness. *If I be wicked, woe unto me, and if I be righte*ous, *yet will I not lift up my head. I am full of confusion, therefore see though my affliction*[10].

Am I righteous or am I wicked, such a grey area at the moment. If I do things I do not want to out of necessity am I still wrong? Is desiring to make love to someone I shouldn't but cannot keep away from wrong? Surely something so good is a gift to be grabbed with both hands even it is only for a short time. If no one is physically hurt is it still a sin? I could argue a side to both parts of the puzzle but would still be no further forward. All the women that must have come through this house, or cellars, must have been so afraid or distressed. They must have known they would not be saved. How cruel the world can be......but is it just sadism?

---

[10] Job 10 v 15

What do the Dragons get out of their perversions, besides the sating of the worst possible carnal desires?

I have never seen money change hands but then I'd always been sent formal invitations. There must be some sort of monetation keeping all the wheels turning. I have not even been aware of any dealings they have had with the bank. What makes such a well oiled machine tick?

I stare out the window at the dimming light and question why I am still 'standing'. How have I survived this far? I have sacrificed everything and it has lead me to a grandiose house acting as a facade for a medieval torture chamber and glorified slave trade. I have not risen in life but been dragged to the gates of hell. How much longer will I survive?

Sometime later I rise from my seat in the now darkened room. I pull the velvet curtains and lighting the candle once more I leave the room.

I head to the kitchen to check on cook, she must still be feeling ill if Lily had been making her tea. Pushing open the door I find cook slumped over the long oak kitchen table, where I had last seen her. She appeared to be sleeping. Shaking her shoulder gently I do not get a response. I do not even know her name........

'Cook?' I shake her a second time.

'Cook?' and a third before I realise that there is no life in the slumped figure. I lift her head from the resting arms and her wide lifeless eyes and contorted face stare up at me.

What has Lily done?

This really should not be my first thought, cook was ill. If I had not seen what I did from my spy hole I would not have doubted this was natural causes or at least due to illness. However, I did see what I should not, now I have my doubts.

Leaving Cook's body sitting at the table I go in search of Lily.

I find her in her bedroom also staring out the windows at the darkness, a dark shapely silhouette in the light of the candles. Despite what I have just seen I want to take her in my arms and forget everything just for a short time. I scold myself at the direction of my thoughts.

'She's dead', I whisper.

'I thought she might be', was the quiet response, but I did not expect the coldness of her voice or the lack of body movement. I thought the news would upset Lily more.

'You must have got to know her these last few days, are you not sorry she has gone?'

'I have seen worse and I am really not going to have time to miss someone I barely knew. She lasted longer than I expected'.

I do not let Lily know that I had seen here making the tea in the kitchen.

'She did not appear to have been as ill yesterday. I thought she just had a stomach complaint. I shall have to inform Samuel of her demise. I am sure they will need to find someone to replace her quickly, someone who will know how to keep secrets and not be missed'.

'Cook had a deep cut in her hand, I thought perhaps she had tetanus due to the severe spasms she was having this morning. She also had that fever for days now.'

Still I say nothing.

'Let Samuel know but tell him I am willing to prepare the food for everyone. My final gift to you all'.

'Gift?'

'Maybe not a gift, but my last supper. Think of your wine as my blood and the food as my body. Eat of my flesh, drink from my soul and toast their good fortunes. Jesus gave his disciples a last supper to remember him. I shall do the same and they shall have a night they will not forget.

Therefore the skilful commander takes up a position in which he cannot be defeated and misses no opportunity to master his enemy[11].

'Are you sure that you can cope with cooking a meal for twelve? Do you remember what happened the other night? I am not convinced my reactions were entirely due to alcohol'.

'I shall plan everything precisely and they will enjoy every mouthful. Just be careful how much of the wine you consume, you may want to have your senses unimpaired. Besides, it shall give me a welcome distraction from thinking about what else shall be happening that evening. In five days time it will all end. Everything'.

'Do not be surprised if this does not work out as you plan. Samuel may still instruct the order of the Cook's death and another stranger may join us here in the next few days........or worse.

We should lay out the cook before we sleep. It may be hard to shift her if rigour sets in'.

I leave her to her thoughts and the flickering candles. She will follow me downstairs......I hope.

Then I must write a letter.

---

[11] Quote from 'The Art of War: New Illustrated edition, by Samuel Griffith, Watkins Publishing, 2001

It is said that to play the fool takes skill and a certain type of wit. In centuries past the court fool or jester would observe the mood of those to whom they would jest, for the wrong word to the wrong person would mean a very unwelcome ending.

A true fool thinks himself wise but a wise man knows himself to be a fool. Contradiction after contradiction.

In our game or should I say readings of tarot, 'The Fool' is a sign of unfulfilled potential, a man about to step off the edge of a cliff, with a dog at his heels warning him of the danger. Ironically he holds a white rose as he begins this journey.

I think if I had my cards read that fateful night in Belfast 'The Fool' would have been drawn. I feel trapped, but yet I have nothing to keep me here....or do I? I have experienced a certain freedom these last few days and don't want to give it up....but I must. Anything else I would choose to do would be a 'fool's errand' Yet I must play the role of fool well, I must indulge my superiors and Lily. Some thoughts are playing havoc with my peace of mind since last night. I am unsure if I am a fool or Lily is playing a very good part.

I so badly want to believe that my eyes deceived me or my imagination is making up stories that aren't really there. My heart wants to believe in the fairy story but my gut is telling me that not all stories have a happy ever after.

I feel confused.

When I was with her last night I could not voice my doubts for fear of hurting her feelings. But, I know what I saw and heard and I so badly want her to tell me the truth without me asking for it.

I wrote to Samuel at dawn and sent the letter directly with the stable boy. I do not like the uncertainty of what may happen today. It is a day to keep busy but I know the waiting will make me idle.

Lily is of course in the kitchen making a mess of weird looking colourful dishes or concoctions. The green tinge to everything looks like she is brewing up some sort of witch's potions.

Why did she have to get that dye from Mrs. Fox?

Every shelf is filled with wild flowers and weeds; dandelions, fox gloves, parsley, mushrooms and berries. Personally I would much rather have potatoes and vegetable broth than dandelion and parsley.

She does seem to be happy in her work. I would be more of a hindrance than a help so I retire to the library and wait for a reply to my letter.

It is after three o clock before the stable boy returns with a response.

Dear Virgil,
It is rather short notice to be able to find a replacement for Mrs. Moore. I will deal with the funeral arrangements,
If the girl wishes to be in charge of the arrangements for her own sacrifice then we shall let her. However, I think it would be wise to return to Belfast and we shall arrange a new venue for the feast. I shall meet with you on your return. Tomorrow evening should be suitable.

Yours SM

There is so much to do before returning to Belfast.

Immediately I go in search of Lily to let her know the new plans.

She does not seem pleased that we are to leave.

'I have been planning what to cook all day Virgil with what I have available here. Where shall I get the same ingredients in the city?'

'Perhaps if you make up a list we can find as much as possible before we leave and take them with us to Belfast. The things should keep for a few days'.

'That is a good idea we should pack what is already here and I will need to go and find more mushrooms, dandelions and elderflower. Do we have any pigeons? If you knew where to find the ingredients we could go and look for them now and pack everything else this evening'.

Lily knows exactly what she requires so at least there will not be any resistance when it comes to leave even she is not entirely happy.

Lifting a couple of baskets from the kitchen we head to the fields at the back of the house. Although only five o'clock now the sun has started to fade and there is a chill in the air.

'It will be a couple of hours yet until it is dark but it is probably best to get the items which are furthest away first'.

Leading the way I head east, away from the house. It is just about a mile to the nearest copse of trees or small forest.

'Hopefully we should find mushrooms and pine seeds in the shade of the trees'.

We walk in silence for a while, more aware of our footing than our conversation. The field is littered with holes from the cows sinking in the damp earth.

I take Lily's hand so we can both have support, it wouldn't do breaking an ankle at this stage. Hopefully it will still be light on the return journey or we may have trouble returning the same path.

Despite the potholes we make our journey within the hour. There are many more trees than I remembered......or maybe they have just grown.

'I haven't been here in years. I think if we take the short cut through the trees. We should be able to get you what you need'.

'I don't know if I can climb over that ditch it looks as if it is deep with mud'.

Throwing the baskets over the ditch first and then jumping over myself, I stretch half way across and grab Lily beneath the arms and swing her over the mud.

Landing in front of me she stumbles and falls against me. Despite all other thoughts in my head regarding her actions all I want to do is kiss her.

I don't resist.

Briefly meeting her eyes with mine I pull her closer arms wrapped around her, I kiss her. Just a brief kiss is not enough. I want more and I want her......here. Lifting the baskets in one hand and taking Lily's hand in the other I move deeper into the darkness under the roof of branches. Throwing the baskets aside I again kiss Lily, her back balanced against the nearest tree. My hand cups her face, my thumb rubs across her lips, she is soft under my rough fingers. I feel one of her hands on my neck pulling my head closer as she responds.

Both sets of hands move southwards, resting on buttocks pulling each other closer, as close as one can get through unnecessary garments. I pull her skirts higher with both hands as I briefly kiss the skin at the top of her bodice. My hands meet the silky tops of her stockings and garters, before finding the flesh above.

No bloomers!

Lily had said she didn't like them restricting her anyway.

My hand moves between her thighs pushing them apart, my fingers searching for warm dampness. Rubbing her clit with my thumb my fingers slowly slide inside her. Pushing upwards, teasing, testing, and checking, if she wants me inside her as much as I want to be there.

She looks me in the eyes as she unbuckles my belt and undoes my button flies. She slides a cold hand into my breaches and searches for an already erect cock. Timidly at first, gently, she strokes me, then harder as her grip tightens and a finger rubs over the fluid at the tip.

I remove my fingers from inside her, meaning to lay her down on the ground. But, before I can guide her she has knelt down in front of me, one hand on my buttocks the other gripping my shaft. She leans forward and takes first the tip of my cock in her mouth. Slowly her tongue flickers, then gently a little more, she pulls me to her with the hand on my buttock as she takes my entire length in her mouth, slowly she moves, the other hand gripping my shaft as she sucks on me.

My legs tremble.

I am shocked and pleasantly surprised. I do not want it to end so quickly.

'Lily stop'.

She looks up at me with her two blue eyes teasing as she still works her devil's magic. My cock in her mouth.

I pull backwards releasing myself from her grip.

'Is something wrong?'

'On the contrary I enjoyed that immensely but I want to feel you and be inside you. I don't want to finish yet'.

Taking off my shirt I lay it on the bed of needles. Laying Lily on top of it I pull her skirts up to her waist and my hands open her legs and I look at her. Taking my cock in my own hand I lie on top of her, guiding myself inside her. My mouth again finding hers, kissing, thrusting, her hands pulling my buttocks so close to her that I cannot go any deeper. She moans slightly...she is getting used to the feel of sex, I feel her tighten her muscles around me pleasuring herself as much as she is pleasuring me.

I hear voices!

I freeze.

They sound far enough away that they would not see us. Lily turns my face to hers and whispers, 'Don't Stop'.

Her eyes bore into me as we move together and I feel her climax as she bites on my chest muffling a scream of pleasure. I cannot hold back any longer. It takes all my will power not to make a sound and I growl as I empty myself into Lily. Trembling I lie on top of her, kissing her forehead.

'Were you not afraid they would hear us?'

'I was too excited I've never felt anything like that before, I didn't want you to stop. I did not care who saw. If it was no one either of us knew it would not matter. All that mattered in that moment was us'.

'In a strange way I liked you telling me not to stop, but I was also scared they would see us. I am not sure where they went to, we should straighten ourselves up and leave'.

She fixes her skirts and rises lifting my shirt, she hands it to me. It is damp where my semen has run out of her. Not much I can do about it now and I can't walk home without a shirt on. That really would get people talking.

The real purpose of the outing needs completing before dark. Taking Lily by the hand I lead her in the direction of the mushrooms and seeds. We fill the basket with quite a few fresh looking button white mushrooms and some darker brown and head back towards the fields and the dandelions, parsley and whatever else she believes she requires. We arrive back at the house just as light vanishes, mission accomplished and rather hungry.

While Lily arranges her provisions and the larder, I cook some potato and soda bread. It will do to 'fill a hole' it's been a while since I had some freshly made with a lot of butter.

Too late to travel now we pack all that we need to return to Belfast. I don't want to sleep on my own tonight; I have a sick feeling in my gut that it will be the last opportunity that I may get to be with Lily.

I knock on the door before entering.

She is already in bed but throws the covers aside to invite me in. I do not feel a lustful urge. I just want to hold her and know that she is near. I do not sleep well that night; mainly because I want to remember every moment.

Dressed, packed and ready to depart on the trip back to Belfast, I take one last look at the house. You never know what the future holds and I want to remember every detail and every magic moment that I have spent these last few weeks.

Lily meets me in the hall carrying the family Bible.

'What do you need that for?'

'Samuel will have no need for it and probably not even notice it is gone. Perhaps it shall bring me some comfort in the days to come'.

Perhaps she is right, but I did not think the Bible was something that Lily would turn to. I think she would be more likely to seek solace in some form of revenge. Then again perhaps I am wrong, what opportunity would there be to take revenge, now, on such powerful men. Let her bring the Bible if that is what she needs.

The journey home does not take long and I am opening my own front door a few hours later. It seems such a long time since I had been here, yet it is only a matter of weeks. Time passed so slowly for years and yet I feel I have filled the last few weeks with more than the last ten years.

I am momentarily embarrassed by the dust and cobwebs. The house may be tidy but I do not remember the last time I dusted and cleaned properly. It has been some time since anyone has been invited over my threshold.

Hopefully Lily will not mind.

It has been even longer since the spare room was used. I throw the door open and open the window to air the space for Lily. She sits down on the metal framed bed and all at once the room is filled with dust particles dancing in the daylight.

'I'll unpack and take the bed clothes out and beat them in the yard and let them hang in the breeze a while. Then perhaps we can go for a walk', she says.

'A walk is just what is needed after the journey, it does get a bit cramped and suffocating in the carriage.

An hour later we are walking through the centre of Belfast, I am avoiding holding Lily's hand or taking her arm in mine. There is quite a bustle about; everyone is looking forward to the weekend. The factories have not yet closed so most of the people we pass are well dressed business men or their wives. We head in the general direction of Queens and Botanic, not having discussed our destination I feel I am unconsciously being lead towards Botanic Gardens.

'Are we going to see the glass house at Botanic?

'Now that we are in this direction perhaps we could.....you did promise to bring me back and this may be the last opportunity'.

'Then that is what we shall do'.

The curved metal and glass structure of The Palm House is open this time and Lily wants to look at every single specimen. How can anyone be so excited about flowers, plants and trees? Politely I nod as she describes the plants and what she knows about them not really hearing a word she is saying. I am glad when we have walked around the entire building and back out in the fresh air.

Taking the path we had taken the previous Sunday afternoon we walk passed the bushes the children had been eating from.

Lily runs her hands along the branches knocking berries to the ground.

'It'll maybe stop the children eating them if they are on the ground', she says.

Completing a circuit of the gardens we head back towards the town, briefly stopping at Kelly's Cellars for a drink. The factories are closed now and the bar is very busy with men in squandering their weekly wages. Too many bodies squashed into the space and no other females. We take the long way home passed the river and a view of the docks.

What a view there is of one of the finest shipyards in the world! Some of the buildings closest to the river have been built on the top of the Black Water River and it still runs through the tunnels beneath their foundations, such a clever way to reclaim land and make more space.

I take Lily's hand now as we amble along the river. There are not many to see us, but there are also not too many well dressed folk in this area and they wouldn't think twice of robbing us.

To the right of us is the river and on the far bank the docks, in front The Custom House, and in the near distance the spire of the new Sincler Seamans Church which was completed just last year.

'I would love to climb aboard one of those boats and never return but then some other woman would be taken in my place. If only things were different and there were no responsibilities to take control of our lives. How different everything could be........a new life in America or Canada, children, a home, dreams and ambitions. A curse is on us if we stay or go, our destinies await'.

'*On either side the river the long fields of barley and of rye. There she weaves by night and day, a magic wel with colours gay, she heard a whisper say, a curse is on her of she stay* ....our dear Lady of Shalott. You are right of course.....cursed whether we stay or go'.

My arm is now placed around Lily in the chill of the early evening air and breeze from the Lough; I pull her closer and kiss her.
Almost immediately she starts beating at her skirts and pulling away.

174

'Something just ran over my feet, I didn't want it running up my legs'.

'It was a rat', I reply as I see the furry creature disappearing into a hole in the mud. I silently curse it for interrupting my kiss.

'I'm not too fond of the furry little fellows myself and would rather not come across another. Let us make home and get some food'.

The moment has passed.

Still flustered Lily pats down the material in her clothes to double check and takes my hand as we walk around 'The Half Bap', to Donegal Street.

Walking towards the house I realise a carriage is pulled up outside. Quickly I let go of Lily's hand as if it burnt me.

She glares at me.

'I forgot Samuel was going to call', I respond to the icy look.

It had totally left my mind that he was going to visit this evening. What a fool! At least there is nothing sitting or in the house to lead suspicions to Lily and I being closer than we should.

'Can you busy yourself in the kitchen while he is here? Maybe make some tea please?'

'Yes, that won't be a problem I am used to making myself invisible......you didn't even realise I lived next door', she smiles.

'Thank you I am grateful'

'How grateful?' she asks while looking like a very beautiful devil in whose hands butter wouldn't melt.

'Behave I need to compose myself!'

We enter the house, Samuel is already inside, it is technically still his house and he has a key.

Immediately I begin to apologise, I did not realise he would call so early.

'I decided to call on close of business as I have other things to attend to this evening. What have you two been up to?' he directs the question at Lily, who has not had the opportunity to pass him in the hall.

'We walked to the Botanic Gardens, I needed something a little special for the feast', she replies her face devoid of any form of expression.

We did not get anything at Botanic........please do not ask what it was. My fingers crossed behind my back.

'What is it?' he asks immediately. I can feel myself start to sweat.

Lily just smiles and says, 'It's a surprise. Wait and see. Is there any chance you could send me some pigeons to prepare over the weekend please?'

He just looks at her a few seconds as if he is unsure how he should react and says 'of course, anything you do prepare will be collected on Monday at noon to transfer to the venue'.

'Thank you, everything will be ready and waiting, the jellies and blancmange will need to be kept cool'. Lily then nods her head and leaves me alone with Samuel.

My hat in my hand I gesture to Samuel to enter the sitting room. We take a seat at each side of the unlit fire.

'I hope everything is going to plan for the feast Virgil? We cannot have any additional problems at this stage'.

'I do not know anything other than I am to look after the girl, and that we will be getting fed'.

'I shall be taking over as master of ceremonies; the elder gentleman you already met became ill just after the soiree at my home. They buried him a few days ago. Although I have no previous knowledge of this ceremony, he has named me as his replacement and left instructions. You can see why no other hiccups can happen in relation to the ceremony. I have not had time to name a new membership secretary either which means no other events can be organised at present without my knowledge of members, addresses, venues, girls etc. We must talk properly after the feast'.

'I am sorry to hear of the gentleman's death but we only briefly met on a few occasions. Am I to understand you wish me to replace you? I do not think I am up to the task or the expectations of the post'. I really want nothing to do with organising those repulsive dinners and orgies, but, how do I refuse without losing my head both figuratively and literally.

'Nonsense! You will be perfect! Most of what you require is at my house in the country. I had planned that you should replace me all along but unfortunately the death of Emily and other unfortunate events and deaths have meant it will be a lot sooner than anticipated. I won't keep you any longer. I just wanted to reassure myself that the girl was ready and that everything shall run smoothly. I need to familiarise myself with the ritual and rites over the weekend.....I shall see you on Monday evening, a coach will collect you both'. Samuel rises to leave barely giving me time to reply. 'I shall see you anon', he continues and lets himself out of the house.

I sit back down on the fireside seat and breathe deeply to steady my nerves. It is strange how even the best laid plans can go awry. Samuel's presence has made the upcoming sacrifice far too real.

I begin to count the hours..............

19th June 1858

The kitchen I have in my house on Donegal Street is adequate for my needs. I cook very little, not because I like to cook, but out of necessity for eating.

At daybreak I am wakened by a crashing sound in the kitchen below. Pulling on my clothes from yesterday I go to investigate. I have few pots and pans but enough that Lily had managed to send them all crashing to the floor.

'Sorry, I was trying to be quiet, and then I tried to pull out the jelly mould from the top shelf and lost my balance'.

'If I had not presumed it was you making the racket I would have presumed we were under attack!'

'Again sorry, I thought I would try and prepare the desserts, wine and soup today so maybe tomorrow we could relax a little.....maybe even go to church? She looks at me with one eyebrow arched and I am not entirely convinced she is being serious. 'If at all possible is there somewhere we could get a sleeping draft or some laudanum? I would like to get some sleep tonight and I am sure in the coming days you will also be in need of a little help, counting sheep will be no use'.

Perhaps she is right, sleep has eluded me these last months more so than it has in years. I do not think I ever really sleep....and maybe never will, but I daren't turn to drugs, but whisky is my Achilles heel. Little slices of death, that break up the long endless days, wake, work, try to sleep and repeat. Nights of endless nightmares induced by love and a loss of faith. If Lily wishes to sleep then we will have to find an emporium or doctor who shall provide what she needs....on a Saturday, It seems to be the fashion for doctors to provide draughts to overwrought women, ,maybe if I do the talking it should be easy enough to obtain.

'Why do you want to sleep? If I thought this was my last few days on earth I would want to fill them with so much, even if I would not need the memories, there is so little time left'.

'Maybe the biggest and best memories are yet to be made. Have faith! The snake may yet swallow its own tail, God may provide a sacrificial lamb, although, I doubt it. We do not know what tomorrow will bring, we just need to open the gate and hope that something good lies beyond. I have not yet given up on hope, no matter how fickle and uncaring she may be. I am not ready to close our box......not just yet, Pandora will be on our side, to help us unleash the demons and carry our enemies to hell. Two more nights to deliver us from the same place, I will not abandon all hope just yet. Two more nights and we will either be delivered from purgatory or be dining with the demons for all eternity.'

'How can you be so hopeful? There is nothing we can do, especially with Samuel attending. He is obsessive he will have left no stone unturned and will have a backup plan for every eventuality; there will be no chance for mistakes'.

'Sometimes organisations destroy themselves from within, all you need is for one domino to fall and the rest will follow. Sometimes, skimmed milk masquerades as cream, and, sometimes, the ides and destiny will be on the side of good. It's time to break the chains surrounding us'.

'How can they destroy themselves? They are strangers walking on egg shells, waiting to walk through coals because a higher power dictates. To disobey is folly and at most death. Even I do not know how to disobey without us both being destroyed. Yet, with you gone, I will be dead anyway. If I knew how to break chains and open gateways I would do it, but I am no wizard, I am just a man who has become a death dealer because I wanted what I had no right to want. I wanted the greener grass, the firmer walls, better living......what has it brought me.....shame, heartache, a cynical and twisted mind.....and others.....I dare not even think what my actions have brought to others, other women, other men, families......my family.....hurt, death, despair, and all for what? An inexperienced fumble on a chaise in a strange living room, with a strange girl I just met. Life can change in an instant. You are also a stranger .....yet....even from the first night it never felt that way. We should have known each other our whole lives.....but we will not. This is not an ending I would ever have anticipated and I am very sorry for the role I will play'.

'Do not despair, just yet, I have everything in hand......I hope'.

I look at her taking in her appearance as she stands still holding the copper moulds. I do not yet know what she has planned but I know she is determined, the stance and defiant look say she will not be easily swayed.

Silence.

'Do you want to get the medicine before or after you cook?'

'Whatever you think best. Are they easy to obtain?'

'I think if I tell the apothecary you have been quite distressed and frantic there should be no problems. However, it is Saturday and the problem will be finding an emporium which is open. We should have breakfast and then go out first, that way if it takes a while we will have the day.

How can someone who has been hidden away their entire lives know so much about the world? You astound me'.

'Go get dressed and washed I shall make breakfast and some of the soups. I may not have had company but the worlds that can be created from books were all I needed.......until now'.

I ascend the stairs with a pitcher of water still curious as to what Lily has planned.

I did not realise there were so few established apothecaries in Belfast. I suppose not everyone can afford medicines the same as if they were to buy food. Eventually we find one open near Castle Street. The door opens with the familiar chime of a bell. It occurs to me that I have very seldom been in shops in Belfast, unless to buy food. Twelve years in one place and I know few of its secrets. The shop smells of incense and various herbal concoctions. I can smell a hint of opium and wonder would it be more beneficial than laudanum.

A tall gentleman in a white shirt and black apron appears from the back of the shop, wiping a pair of spectacles on his apron as he appears.

'How can I be of assistance, sir, madam?'

'Would it be possible to get something to help someone sleep quicker and for longer? Lily asks. 'I've been very distracted lately and my poor husband is not entirely pleased with getting no sleep'.

'Certainly I can give you something herbal or some laudanum'.

'I have already tried lots of herbal remedies as we are from the country and they were easily obtainable unfortunately some take a while to work and others had no effect. Something that acts quickly would be preferable to lying awake for hours'.

The man turns to the selection of large stoneware jars and selects a couple; he pours the contents into a smaller glass bottle.

'That should keep you going a while madam that will be eight shillings please'.

I hand the gentleman a couple of bank notes and thank him for his service before leaving.

'Is there anything else you require before we go back home?' I ask Lily

'Can we call at the greengrocers and I need a marrow bone to use for the blancmange, which would be everything'.

We call at the outdoor stalls at St.George's Market and go home.

Lily spent most of the afternoon in the kitchen making all sorts of blancmange and weird jellies in all manner of colours. Cooking is definitely an art form and for someone who has never cooked to pick it up so quickly is astonishing. The blancmanges especially are so delicate and hard to make and decorate.

'You will need to put these in the cool house or they shall be melted by Monday evening'.

'They should be fine if I replace the moulds and place upside down in cold water'.

I watch her potter around for a while before returning to the living room. I like to be the voyeur but in some ways it seems such a waste of time that could be spent doing something more memorable.

I cannot settle to read and I spend a good deal of time staring into space my thoughts moving in circles.

Some hours later I hear Lily upstairs and think it is about time I moved from fireside seat. Stiffly I rise to go and see what she is up to.

Lily is in her room, the red velvet dress, corset and stockings all laid on the top of the bed. She is standing her back to me wearing nothing but her linen blouse just about covering her buttocks.

I am instantly aroused.

'Will you help me dress? Lily smiles.

'If I must. You look just fine as you are!'

Lifting the corset I place it around her middle, fastening the hooks at the back, I slowly draw the ties tighter before crossing the ribbons again around the middle, my hands either side of her waist and securing at the front.

I lift her hair moving it to one side of her neck; my hands touch her shoulders and leaning closer I inhale the smell of her skin, her hair, the smell of lavender beneath the hint of food. Briefly I bury my face in her hair and feel her closeness before lifting the stockings from the bed.

She sits.

Kneeling I roll the delicate silk in my hands and gently roll the stocking up her foot, over her ankle, her legs slightly apart displaying everything that I would reach as I slowly ascend, before fastening the first stocking to her suspenders. I repeat the task on her other leg wrapping her in a coat of red. My hands rest on each knee my eyes reach hers.......she lies back on the bed......inviting....permitting me to push her legs apart and bury my head between them. My fingers spread her open as my tongue touches her.....gently teasing....slowly I insert one finger, then two, her hips undulating against them as she rides. Quickening......my tongue flickering faster......she moans......my fingers slick with juices I remove them.....and taste her. Pushing myself up, I stand and remove my trousers, my erect cock standing at attention as it escapes the confines of the material......with one swift thrust I fill her....she gasps....ready but not expecting my full girth. Her legs surround me grasping me around the back pinning me to her, pulling me into her, her hands on my buttocks, deeper, I cannot thrust....I am so deep within her. She moves her hips again holding my cock in a vice like grip, slowly clenching and unclenching her muscles.

I kiss Lily our tongues imitating the dance the rest of our bodies are performing, as she sucks on my tongue and bites my lip. Pushing up on my arms I look down on her. Her legs unclasp me and I thrust into her, long, hard, slow strokes, faster, I cannot hold back any longer as I spend myself inside her. I do not withdraw but prop myself on one elbow looking into her face, a hand tracing a line on her now rosy cheeks. She kisses my fingers and smiles.

'I should definitely have preferred your services as a tailor to that of Mrs. Fox'.

'We aim to please madam.....do you still want to get dressed?' I ask hoping that we can remain in bed for the rest of the evening.

'I think everything is in order, you can undress me again and wait until Monday to see the rest of my attire. We should have a lot to ask God to forgive us for at church tomorrow'.

'I didn't think you were serious about attending a service'.

'I have never been I should like to be introduced to the God that has deserted me. Maybe he will hear our prayers'.

20th June 1858

The sleeping draught was not required last night. There was not much sleep had anyway, but what the short hours of night had in store was much preferred. I have never before spent the night wrapped in someone else's limbs, encased in linen shrouds, exploring, learning, desiring, wanton, our bodies joined as one. Some memories are there to be remembered, reminisced, replayed, felt; some memories can never die no matter how much they hurt.

1883

I close my eyes and see her now kneeling before me.....the top of her red hair shining in the moonlight. My green wingback chair sits in the midst of a forest clearing, a circle of light surrounded by shadows. I feel her touch, her lips, her hands, the top of her head.....I hear the voices in the distance; they are nearly here, growing closer, coming out of the shadows. Yet I hear my own voice whisper, 'don't stop'.

'Don't stop'.

A mix of pleasure and of pain and the ecstasy of the real and the unfed desires. These dreams feed my days they nourish my soul they have kept me alive these last years. I cannot give into the shadows; if I did she would vanish forever.

1858

Untangling the limbs and shrouds, I rise; Lily moans quietly beside me, half awake. It is not early and if she wants to attend a Sunday service she will need to rise and wash. We cannot go to church smelling of sin.

I shake her gently.

'Lily, time to get up, you can lie if you wish but if you still want to go to church you will have to rise'.

'Yes', she moans, 'I do'.

'The bath is in the kitchen if you fill it while I make breakfast then we can wash and eat. Service will be at ten o'clock. It's not as late as country services there are not too many farmers in the town needing to feed livestock'.

Dressed maybe not entirely appropriately for church we make our way across to Sincler Seamans. The church was only finished the year previously and the inside of the building still smells of new wood and varnish. It is a bit of a contrast to the hundred year old dust and mildew of the old country presbytery. The inside of the building resembles that of the inside of a boat with the minister at the stern of the vessel; captain to his flock, a flock mostly consisting of dock workers and their families, dressed in their Sunday best shirts and various shades of fawn and grey clothing.

When we had chosen Lily's clothes they had not been intended for church. She sticks out like a sore thumb in her blue velvet corset and dress. Perhaps if we had been thinking we should have gone next door for her old servants clothes. Hindsight is a great thing. I imagine they think her my whore dressed as she is in such bright colours. Perhaps though she could be thought of as a penitent whore seeking God's guidance.

God forgive me for thinking such things of her as I would strike anyone who had said or suggested the same.

We take a seat at the back.

I forget my origins nowadays, I should have had more thought and realised that most of the congregation would have been working class. The guilt of my current station in life eats at my soul and the service has not yet begun.

A tall thin minister of around my own age stands at the pulpit. He invites us to join him in singing hymn 256, 'Will your anchor hold in the storms of life, when the *clouds unfold their wings of strife, when the strong tides lift and the cables strain will your anchor drift or firm remain........'.* It is such a long time since those words crossed my lips, when they were sung from rote at church or Sunday School. They are appropriate and evocative, my anchor and cable are strained to their limit in the current storm, but drifting is not an option.

Lily gently squeezes my hand in her gloved one as we stand; me singing, her listening. The final cadence sounds and we all sit.

'Brothers and sisters we are gathered here on this crisp summer's morning. God has given us such glorious weather these last weeks, weather for work, for safe sailing, planting seeds, growing flowers. This time of the year fills our lives with so many colours and a joy of life......I'm sure you will all agree it lifts the soul to see such a glorious countryside.

Only this morning I looked out the window at the Cavehill and wondered that such a view could be fashioned by fire and brimstone, fires as strong as hell itself. Yet look at it now and how it has changed over the centuries. We also can be delivered from the flames and returned to the path of God.....for we are all sinners, each and every one of us. It is important to ask God to forgive our sins and to be born again in Christ, when we are filled with temptation, lust, greed we must turn from these thoughts. We must reject the fruit of evil, Deuteronomy 32 verse 32 states *For their wine is from the wine of Sodom and the fields of Gomorrah their grapes are grapes of poison their clusters, bitter.* How great are your sins? How have you reacted to temptation? Do you ask for the will power to turn away from Satan or the power of God's forgiveness? Not all fruit is sweet and just one bad apple can poison the soul for eternity. You must ask God into your soul today, use our lives to serve him'

Why do I feel that every word has been written just for me? It was not always the case. I used to listen and not hear. Today I am listening to the sermon and wondering how it would be possible to reject my current predicament. All I can muster is that God will provide what I need......but not what I want. How?

We bow our heads in prayer and listen to the minster's final words. Lily and I remain seated until most have left. I can see she is taking in every part of her surroundings. It is an interesting building and design, the mast of the ship resembling the cross.

Standing we join the procession out of the building, shaking the minister's hand as we leave.

The sun is shining on us as we walk back towards the house. Such a glorious day. 'What did you think of the service?

'I am not sure. It is as if everything is supposed to scare you into submission to worship. He talked of glorious weather and thanks, yet it all can turn to a metaphorical darkness as life's troubles encourage men to sin. What is sin? Why is one man's salvation another's downfall? It felt like the only reason God should be obeyed is because we face death otherwise. Everything that should be enjoyed or valued in life is wrong and we should be punished for loving, living, drinking, eating; everything is a sin. Give up everything that is enjoyable to thank God for making everyone miserable? I am already miserable.....so I doubt he is going to be of much comfort and I face my death already'.

'In truth I find not much comfort in my religious upbringing, how can such an omnipotent being allow pain, murder, betrayal, slavery? If he is so good; why does earth resemble hell? If he is so powerful why does everyone not love one another and live in an eternal state of bliss? The reason we would be told is that we must seek forgiveness for our sins to earn our place in heaven. Why put sin there in the first place.....God the creator of all created sin in some way when the devil fell from heaven.

Everything confuses me these days....and tomorrow we must pay our tithes to yet another God of whom I do not know. Surely you can see why I have lost my faith in humanity'.

'Maybe it was not such a great plan to go to church, I just thought maybe I could ask forgiveness for my sins....and I did. What shall we do with the rest of today? This time tomorrow we shall be preparing for an ending'.

'How about you go and put on some older clothes and we take a walk up the Cavehill. Apparently it's probably the only place we will not be burnt alive today. I've never been up to the caves before and we might as well do something neither of us has ever experienced'.

I did not realise it was such a distance to the grounds of Belfast Castle; it took a couple of hours to walk that distance before starting to climb up the hill. Walking through the trees was peaceful and despite the good weather not many people were about; perhaps keeping the Sabbath, Holy, unlike us.

We reached the caves and realised that we would have to climb straight up the cliff face into the first cave, The only way Lily was going to manage it was to remove her skirt, as she could not even tuck it in her bloomers as she was wearing no underwear again.

I am thankful there does not appear to be anyone about for miles, however, I dread to think of the mariners enjoying their Sunday lunch and doing some 'bird watching' through a telescope or pair of binoculars. It would certainly give them something to discuss over dessert, if they caught an eyeful of Lily's white ass ascending the rocks. Definitely not very lady like but she insisted she was not going to miss out because of a lack of material, or rather too much of it.

I grab her hand as she finally reaches the mouth of the cave.

It is not as deep as I had expected and very dirty, empty ale bottles litter the floor and it smells of urine. Surely our predecessors could just have relieved themselves over the edge. No chance of any naughty or lustful thoughts despite Lily's hourglass silhouette in the mouth of the cave; a blacked out canvas over a sunlit Belfast.

'What do you think they use this cave for?' she asks, 'drinking, smuggling, pirates, a look out for ships? If it were clean,' she sniffs, 'we could hide here, and surely no one would look'.

'A great idea! Except the whole of Belfast just saw the Lily white ass of a harlot climbing the face of the Cavehill', I tease, 'you will be on the front page of *The Northern Whig* tomorrow. Just do not say God made you do it....that you wished to experience his divine work for yourself'.

'Nobody saw..... it's like the window to a castle in the sky looking out over the whole of the Lough and town, I bet at night you could almost touch the stars'.

'Perhaps but we cannot stay until dark it would be too dangerous to get down'.

We sit in silence a good while, our legs hanging over the edge, watching the world pass us by and boats sailing in the distance, her head resting on my shoulder, her hand in mine, no sounds only the beating of our hearts and slow steady breaths.
It is late when we finally descend as far as the castle grounds again, time passed us by without us even noticing. The Sun had begun to set over the mountain.....such a sky! I had never seen anything like it nor seen anything like it since, it ran red like blood. Eventually looking like Belfast was on fire, a good omen or a bad? The shepherds would say tomorrow would be a good day....I am not so sure.

I turn on the tap slowly, I hear a rumbling from the pipes as the pressure builds.....it spurts from the faucet covering me in a flood of red....instantly my home is filled with a sea of blood, I open the front door to let it out into the street....a never ending river....the curse of the Gods and the sky meets the river and it is like drowning in blood and lightning. Where does it come from? I search for the source and find Lily floating above her bed; eyes open wide, eight swords piercing her. Like the origins of a spring the blood babbles from her lips. I can barely hear her voice as the flames and floods engulf us, 'I can still smell the smoke'.

Not yet! Not like this! It cannot end.....

I am pinned down, unable to move; I fight the force, and turn my head towards the voice, 'Virgil, Virgil'.

I wake to find Lily pinning my arms to the bed. I am covered in a cold sweat and my heart hammers so loud my ears are ringing.

'Virgil calm yourself! It was just a dream!'

'I can still smell the smoke....'.

She tilts her head slightly and gives me a strange look but says nothing more. I look at the bedside clock and find it is only just gone seven thirty.

In less than five hours we will be on the final journey.

Lily is already out of bed; still in her night clothes she leaves the room. It is some time before I pull myself together enough to remove myself from the linen sheets. I go to my own room and open the closet. It smells dusty and it is less than a month since it was last opened, a lack of air can suffocate even clothes.

I pull out the shelves and select cufflinks and collar studs. I lift a collar from the circular box and a green silk cravat from the shelf below. My braces I choose to match the cravat then a starched cotton round bottom shirt. Lastly I choose my charcoal grey double breasted dinner tails....which I think make me look like a butler, but I do not wish to wear all black. The clothes selected I lift the tin of polish from its box below my bed and shine my shoes until I could see my face in them.

Everything is ready.

In the kitchen Lily is writing out a list and checking everything is in order. I can smell cooking and realise she has the pigeons Samuel has sent in the oven.

'Are you sure you have enough food? There will only be thirteen including yourself and I shall probably not feel like eating'.

'I want to be sure there is something for everyone so that no one feels left out, besides there are eight courses and plenty of time for nibbling.

MENU

Course 1: Roast mushroom, parsnip and mustard

Course 2: Dandelion and Parsley soup

Course 3: Claret Jelly (claret lemon juice, loaf sugar, whites and shells of 2 eggs, cochineal)

Course 4: Pigeon Compote (pigeons trussed as for boiling, grate crumbs of loaf, pound of bacon fat, thyme, parsley, onion and lemon peel, nutmeg, salt, pepper and 2 eggs)

Course 5: Blancmanges

Course 6: Cakes

Course 7: Liquor, cheese and wine

Course 8: Toasting wine

I have everything under control as far as the preparation is concerned. I just need to double check the wine and juices. I have marked a couple of stronger bottles with an X so if you are being served make sure you do not choose them. I really do not think I could cope with a repeat incident of you running around as if insane'.

'Why did you just not make them all the same it would have been easier'.

'Maybe I would prefer them to be too drunk to remember to drink my blood'.

'I suppose that is very true; eleven insane men would be harder to deal with than one'.

'I shall manage, I am well prepared, and after all I have had almost half my life to be ready for this day'.

'That is true.....yet I have had barely a few weeks and I think if I were in your situation and would never be prepared'.

'Preparation is everything, trust me, it is not the time you have but the situation you find yourself in which will determine any outcome'.

'I shall take your word for it, I feel physically sick not knowing entirely what will happen at the ceremony. I should have asked Samuel for more details'.

'It is best you didn't, not knowing is sometimes better than knowing'.

Once the food is prepared and we have a late breakfast, Lily and I retire separately to dress.

Lily takes a lot longer than expected but I suppose she needed time to herself and her thoughts.

I wait for her in the living room beside the unlit fire. I hear her descent down the staircase before I see her. I rise to greet her and find myself almost speechless at the sight of her in the red attire. My heart pounds, my trousers tighten and my hands sweat, I can barely enunciate my words. 'You look beautiful, like you should be royalty and not merely the sacrificial lamb'.

I take my face in my hands and kiss her......I do not wish it to end but it must....and it is probably our last opportunity to touch, to acknowledge each other.....to feel.

The sound of the door knocking makes us jump apart for it sounds like a drum issuing the death knell. She grabs my wrist as I go to the door, 'You forgot this', she whispers as she hands me the baphomet dagger.

I wish now I had taken the opportunity to say more......I should have told her that I loved her.....Time has finally beaten us.

I open the door.

The coach driver blindfolds us.

I am now more anxious and I do not know what to do or think. I spend the coach journey fidgeting and listening to my own erratic breath inside the cloth.

The journey is very brief and we could not have travelled far. I am most definitely sure we are still within a few streets of Belfast City Centre.

I step sheepishly out of the carriage unsure of my footing as I still cannot see.

'Just through these doors sir', a voice states.

I am guided into the building and left, after a few minutes I remove the blindfold.

I find myself standing in a Grecian style hallway, the walls supported by Corinthian pillars and a ceiling made entirely of stained glass, depicting a woman being tormented by a dragon. There are no other doors in the hall and one set of stairs descending into the bowels of the earth. There seems no other option but to descend into hell.

Another set of stone steps just like that at the house. These are a lot longer and lined with candle lanterns. I must have descended at least three storeys before the stairs come to an end at a large double oak door. I pull the large brass handle towards me.

My mouth opens as I stare in disbelief at what lies before me. I have entered a long room and at first appearance it resembles the body of a church. Despite the ornamental touches the walls are thick with tree roots and moist with condensation. There is a Tudor style ceiling; tiny white and blue mosaic tiles cover the floor in a chequered pattern. In front of me is a long rosewood dining table, with talloned feet, not unlike the usual lions claw detailing, there is a long linen table cloth along the table set with dinner settings and a couple of large candelabras. Behind the table, or in front of it is what could only be described as a baptismal font, made of stone and carved in the most intricate detail, beside that is a communion table draped in red velvet and resembling an altar. In the centre of the red velvet stands a gold chalice.

A stranger may be forgiven for assuming this would be a Christian ceremony; if it were not for the inverted cross on the wall at the very front. A large dragon entwines the cross, its body so detailed, its claws so sharp, it looks lifelike enough to set fire to the room. A fire is lit in the grate just below the head, throwing both light and heat into the surrounding area.

I feel myself begin to shake as I stand in the doorway, one hand covers the other and I take a step backwards. The enormity of the situation hits me and the room begins to spin as I find myself in a state of shock.

I fight back the nausea and try to steady my breath.

Remaining on my feet, barely, I breathe deeply; finding a rhythm I regulate my heartbeat.

I am not entirely sure what I can touch, or look at, I feel like a child in a shop and my mother's back is turned. Should I even be in here? Maybe I should have waited in the hall........where have they taken Lily?

It seems like a very long time before I hear voices, but they do not come from the door. They sound as if they are coming from the fireplace at the front. In a matter of minutes the whole front section of the room rotates to reveal Samuel and Lily and several trolleys filled with food and wine. I move to help them.

'If you help wheel these trolleys forward the girl can begin her work and I can rest the doorway'. Samuel says as he moves towards me.

I push the trolleys towards the table so there is enough space for the font and table when they again rotate. I hadn't been quick enough to see if I recognised any of the fixtures in the adjacent room.

Lily begins to set the food on the table while I decide to question Samuel about what will happen in the ceremony.

'What exactly will this sacrifice and ceremony consist of?'

'We shall take our meal first and then toast our God Abaddon, when the meal and wine are finished we shall prepare the sacrifice. Her hands and throat shall be bled into the font; I shall use the sacrificial knife I am presuming you brought. We perform the ritual and burn her remains in the fire'.

I no longer care that my face probably displays my reaction to the horror which he describes. What sane person could possibly believe that anything good could come from worshipping an obscure deity and drinking blood? I did not think we were Vikings......at least there was no mention of rape.

How can I stop this? Lily is setting the food out oblivious to everything else. Why is she not putting up a fight or trying to escape?

'When will this happen?'

'The others are being delivered as we speak, then we shall commence'.

ϕ

Lily stands in front of the altar, still fully clothed, there shall be no Bacchanalian nymphs at this feast; just a High Priestess watching over the proceedings.

Samuel rises to his feet and addresses the company, 'Brethren we are gathered here to worship and sacrifice. We the chosen few shall present our Lord with his bride. She willingly awaits his arrival and gives freely of her life so that we may feed his soul. Eat and drink, glorify for mit blod und gehorsam we have earned this honour'.

Samuel sits and we all begin to devour our meal while Lily decants the beverages. I avoid the mushrooms as I do not want to be fighting off imaginary demons.

'Who is the God?' I ask Samuel.

'I can understand secrecy given to the woman and all that happens at other events, but do these men even know what they are taking part in? Were they aware they were worshipping a God, or are they just sadists? I presume most are handpicked because of their personalities but I still do not understand why you chose me'.

'In an Old Kingdom Pyramid[12] text the King our Lord orders there to be sacrifices, he alone controls the deaths, he needs humans to feed himself as a God and presents them on an altar, the agents of the King/ God do his bidding, they provide the offerings and as the King eats their magic, he gulps down their souls. The adult souls he prefers for breakfast. Abaddon is an old world God who weighs our souls to find us worthy of serving him in the next life'.

'Did you know all these things before the elder gentleman died?'

'Yes, but my family have served for centuries. It is only as the world changes, justice, crime, society that we have had to take to the shadows. Few of the original families remain. I am the last of my line; each man here only the first of theirs. The bloodline ended with your son's death. You are the only heir to the Orders secrets in this country. We shall discuss all of this tomorrow as planned'.

Samuel eats a few mushrooms and demands more wine.

---

[12] According to Jacob Rabinowitz

I take only a few spoonfuls of soup, it is not to my taste and have not much of an appetite.

The Claret Jelly is served with the Pigeon Compote. A few of the men at the end of the table appear to have drunk too much already, their voices raised in consternation; while opposite me a tall gentleman with a handlebar moustache yawns openly. I try to block out the uproar but the sound of a chair hitting the floor makes it difficult to ignore.

I look at the men and back at Samuel, he does not look pleased. Rising from his seat he heads to the other end of the room, to break up the fighting; he gets punched in the face for his troubles.

I look at Lily still standing at the altar her face passive and she is acting is if nothing is wrong. Personally I think they have probably reacted to the mushrooms. I can hear Samuel asking the other men to hold them, two men on each of the trouble makers. Samuel dispatches them with a swipe of his switch, pulls out his handkerchief and nonchalantly wipes the blade before tucking his napkin under his chin and contriving to eat.

Ten remain.

'Not an ideal situation', Samuel muffles between bites, 'but obviously wrongly chosen'.

I manage to eat a little of the pigeon but it is hard to swallow in my state of shock.

The man opposite me continues to yawn.

Time passes slowly but I presume about an hour between courses four and five. The man opposite has been sleeping for some time and Samuel has not passed comment. He just asked repeatedly for more wine. Lily brings more bottles.

I whisper, 'why are they all so thirsty?'

'Maybe I over salted the food', is her reply.

The man on my right begins laughing to himself like a mad man.

'What do you find amusing?'

'The Fairies, can you not see them sitting on the table nibbling at the cake? Sneaky little critters! My mother used to always say if you caught one it had to grant you anything you wished for; there is a good few hiding at the minute. I'm laughing because nobody else has noticed and I'll have more wishes than Ali Baba did when he found that lamp'.

Raising my eyebrows, 'Good luck to you on catching one'.

I turn to Samuel.

'Has the ceremony always been the same?'

'In the old days everything was more open, we burnt women publicly often under the guise of witchcraft, torture chambers provided the ideal locations for our sacred rituals. Inquisitions, crusades, plague and war all kept us hidden. We were many, legions of us throughout the earth.

Now we are few.

Numbers are irrelevant as long as the ritual continues; which is probably just as well as there has been too much drink I fear. I may have to see off a few more of our companions'.

His eyes fall on another man at the far end of the table who is making a lot of strange shapes with his face and his hands outstretched as if he cannot see.

Samuel once more rises from the seat and removes the switch from his breast pocket. He pulls the gentleman's head back and in the manner of Sweeney Todd dispatches him to join his brethren.

Nine.

The gentleman to the right grabs Samuel by the arm and in his inebriated state asks, 'Was that necessary.....he obviously couldn't handle his wine?'

Samuel places one hand on his shoulder, 'You are of course right, maybe I was a little hasty', he starts to walk back towards his seat, changes his mind and turns back towards the other gentleman. 'However, you have just questioned my judgement and that is not allowed'.

This time he faces the man and with one swift move of his arm almost completely decapitates him. The arterial spray covers the table.

Eight.
'Don't kill the fairies!' the seat beside me is pushed back and the fat little man starts swiping his arms across the table. 'Where did they go? Come on little men come back'.

His face reddens as his temper rises.

He looks at Samuel, 'You made them leave!'

He mounts the table and takes a leap off the table at the other side at Samuel. Food, cutlery, glasses, wine and cloth all follow him.

Chaos ensues.

The other men try to drag him off Samuel.......fists fly.

The man opposite me now rests face first in his soup. I look at Lily, still unfazed standing at the altar. Leaving my seat I approach her.

'What have you done?'

'Thus those skilled at making the enemy move do so by creating a situation to which he must conform. They entice him with something he is certain to take, and with lives of ostensible profit they await him in strength. 'The Art of War' has been very useful. I suggest you stay to the sidelines, Samuel has found a lust for blood tonight'.

I turn around to find Samuel holding the 'Fairy King's; head in his hands, grinning insanely as if he had his own face slit from ear to ear. Happy at his bloody mayhem.

Six.

Another two men lie to his side.

Four.

There was only supposed to be one death tonight. I suppose I should be grateful she is one of only few left standing.

Samuel stands up and grabs hold of the table, he pulls what remains of its contents to the floor before placing the head in the centre....seven more follow as he carves them off their bodies.

'Burn them!' he orders the two other remaining members. They drag the now blood soaked frames one by one across the mosaic floor. The white tiles now black with a sea of blood. I pinch myself to check I am not having another dream.

I wretch and the little I ate leaves my stomach. I do not know what to think; my right hand reaches for a wine bottle. Uncorking it......I drink. Lily swipes the bottle from my hands, 'Do not drink! This is not over'. She removes the knife from my inside pocket and plunges it into the man closest to her as he drags the last body to the flames, pushing him into the fire after the headless corpse.

Three.

The other man grabs her by the throat. I try to separate them but I find my strength is gone. Samuel having heard the ruckus; drags himself away from his death heads.....rather reluctantly. 'Not the girl, you must not harm the girl!'

The man lifts his head from Lily for a few seconds, just long enough for Lily to plunge the dagger into his stomach.

She steps back her face distorted in pain as she realises what she has done; visibly shaking, I guide her away as the body slumps to the floor.

Two.

I hand Lily the wine bottle and she drinks......removing it from her lips she looks at the table, 'What have I done?'

Samuel is not yet finished.

He looks at Lily his blood lust heightened. He removed his dinner jacket throwing it on the floor behind him.

'It is time'.

I find myself unsteady on my feet.

I barely hear Samuel tell her to undress.

Lily removes her corset, her skirt, her bodice, her stockings......I fall to my knees in the sticky mess behind the altar. Samuel hands Lily a rose which she holds in her hands outstretched above her head just over the font.

My eyes meet hers.

She looks frail.....vulnerable.......scared.

A tear roles down her cheek.

'I will glorify thee before the moon of God Abaddon. On snakes, cornfields and vines I will glorify thee, before him who is upon the throne who cannot be destroyed, in whose hand is thy staff'. Samuel's voice drones in the background.

'Virgil' she whispers as her eyes widen and flicker shut, the rose falls from her hand......

'Let his voice be heard. Behold the sacrifice of the flame of the rose'.

I reach for Samuel's jacket and remove the switch....

'Take this our offering to nourish and multiply'.

Samuel raises his hands above his head as if he would plunge the knife into Lily's heart.......I grab his legs for I have not the energy to stand. He bangs his head on the altar and lands beside me unconscious.......In one silent move I finish it.....I slit his throat. I have barely the energy to move......the last thing I see is Lily on the altar; eyes closed resembling her idol Ophelia her flowers now removed. My eyes are heavy; I cannot hold them open......

$$\phi$$

The next day I woke up in my bed.

I never knew how I got home.

It was almost as if it had all been a dream.

1883

Proverbs 22 v 14, The obscene filthy tongue will at length be quiet, in the land of silence and grim death embracing the body in its cold arms, will effectually ally the heart of all fleshly lusts.

I sit in my fading green leather wingback armchair at the side of the fire gazing out the window, one of my hands cupping the whisky glass the other rubbing a hole in the other arm of the chair. My memories are as clear as if it was yesterday, the years having in no way diminished my feelings or emotions. I can close my eyes and still see the look in her eyes as the rose fell from her bloodied hand, the smell of her skin lingering in my nostrils and her voice whispering my name. Every moment treasured and retained, every conversation and movement engraved on my memory. All lost within the labyrinth of this now twisted mind.

Setting the now empty whisky glass on the side table I rise from my seat and I gaze at the painting on the wall before I pull out the drawer of the davenport writing desk. I open the bible still almost unread unlike the pages which it contains. Now fragile and foxed with age I remove the individual leafs of paper from their concealed position. Each time I have read her words over the last years the letter always brings me some new information, some new emotion. Each time it is just as the first time and the pain just as raw. Yet I read them to be close to her, for her words and the painting are all I have left ....other than my memories. Each day I ask myself how was it possible that I only knew Lily for less than a month and yet she has influenced every action, thought and feeling I have experienced since. She still fills my thoughts every second of every day. Apparently time heals all wounds, scars fade and memories disappear. The memories of Lily are so deeply etched within my mind, and on my heart and soul that time will never erase them.

There are days when the dull ache in my chest no longer roars….it fades to a silent whimper….clutching on to the long ago memories. There are days when I remember the wolves no longer howl and all I am left with is the sound of the moon. I may no longer be a stag in heat but my soul still burns I still yearn for her touch and every thought sets me on fire. I can still smell her scent fresher than that of my newly laundered clothes. It is like uncorking a bottle of fine wine or a long distilled whisky and each time I remove the cork it is like being there again in that moment. The first breath, the first taste, the first spark……each memory an accelerant and I am powerless as they flame.

I relive every moment of that night time and time again, every word, every movement, every unsaid thought, every look in her eyes and I feel every emotion and touch as if it is happening again in the present.

The fire was lit in the grate of the drawing room to ward off the coolness that is caused by the thick stone walls. In the very room where *in a sea of folly tossed my choicest hours of life were lost.*[13]

I find that I am no longer pained at my choice. If I had not made the decisions which I had in my youthful madness I would not have met Lily. I would not have journeyed the path which has brought me to my ultimate destination for I am now at the place that fate intended. There is no point in wishing we had met sooner or under different circumstances.

The only regret I have is that I could not lay her to rest; I could not kneel and mourn at her grave. I have often walked through the local graveyard; it somehow makes me feel closer to her. Talking to the tombstones of the dead has been comparable to dealing with the living in latter years. I never knew what happened to her, I turned my back and walked away. I left her there exposed on the altar of red velvet surrounded by the very souls who would have harmed her. Yet in the end she finally found the reason for her education and despite not knowing her parents the love of botany gave her an escape. If only I had her strength I could

---

[13] pope

have cast aside the chains of life before now. Instead I pay my penance and hope that I will not have much longer to wait. Now I know that she would be laid to rest I can find a peace of sorts until we meet again.

Dear Virgil,

Please do not think me a coward. My decision has not been easy. I have never wanted to live as much as I do now in this moment, to feel your hand in mine, your skin, your touch and know, just know that you are mine. I want to kiss the sea and never give into the thirst, to feel your seed inside me and know that a part of you exists in me. It is because you give me life that I must make this sacrifice. It is either me or us both and I could not bear for you to suffer because of me. Please forgive me, and know that I have never wanted anything but you. Know that if I only had one wish and I know it can't come true, I still wish to spend one night in your company.

Do not be sad or angry for the time we spent together had so much substance that it would take anyone else a lifetime to live it. I am sorry that this time was brief but I would live it all again in a heartbeat.

A robin flew in my window this morning it landed on the acorn shaped bed knob at the foot of the bed. It was a fat little fellow his head moving to and fro, its inquisitive eyes taking in every detail. I am unsure if he was a messenger from God or the devil, foretelling his omen of death. His feathered breast so red he must have quenched the thirst of many a sinner in hell. Perhaps at the end God has intervened...... I have my doubts. I made a wish as I lay there watching the movements of the robin. If I were given the same wish again and knew it could never come true I would still wish for the same thing.

I have always been a grounded person when it comes to reality and responsibilities; I never let myself become distracted from the things which I was supposed to be focussed on, until I met you. My early years were spent in the company of older women and men. On reflection I feel that this is why on the few occasions that I socialised I sensed I was born in the wrong time. I have nothing in common with those my own age, women despise me; I do not know why..... and men.......they have always used me although not in the worst of ways. A figure to be lusted after, lorded over, to serve and be served. Please do not think me a narcissist I am merely stating my existence as I have experienced it.

I have been cultivated and educated to such an extent that I live for my books, the smell, the touch, the feel and the images they create in my mind. I do not know the purpose for which I have been educated but I do know if I were ignorant I would question less. I have my own thoughts and perceptions of my purpose. I have always queried my raison d'être yet I have always failed to see my way out. The Dragons are many and I am but one person. Like a spider in a cup I scramble daily to find a way out but even though I can see it, I can never reach it. If I were a sheep I fear I should find it wearisome, mindlessly following the words of others without question. Yet the price of being a wolf is loneliness to choose between one or the other has its own price. I am alone in the labyrinth of my mind exploring different paths and searching for an unlocked door. Each day had a purpose but no substance until I met you.

When my eyes first saw you on the landing at the cartomancy evening it was like a surge of energy filled my body. Once our eyes met that is where it began for me and there was no turning back. You walked away from the table that night, and despite our overly polite tete a tete I wanted nothing more than to see you again. When we met the following evening I knew it was not by accident. After conversing for hours on acting, art literature and books I believed it was not chance, but fate. Fate brought you into my life and my heart. I have never had the opportunity to converse, laugh and love with anyone like you, everything about you appealed to me. The very depths of your soul were laid bare in the pool of your eyes. The hours which we spent seemed to pass in a matter of minutes. If there had been an opportunity to talk all night......I would have taken it. It was a rare pleasure for me and I valued every moment of your company. The feelings that developed that evening have grown considerably. You have no idea how fast my heart beats when I think of you. I have never been in love but if this is what it feels like I would gladly follow you to the bowels of hell, if that is what it took to be with you.

Close your eyes, my time has come
You'll wake up in a while, don't fight the sleep.
Then the methods of my madness will repair your dying soul
I do not wish you to live your life thrown in a corner
Left, forgotten, it's time to rescue you from hell[14]

You can be sure we will meet again for I do believe in reincarnation, that we only have one soul mate through our many lifetimes. Perhaps in the next life we will not just meet and die. Perhaps then we shall live.

Till we meet again, I will always be yours

Lily

---

[14] Words from Stormzone, 'Seven Sins' album used with permission of J. Harbinson.

Printed in Poland
by Amazon Fulfillment
Poland Sp. z o.o., Wrocław